Almost
FRIENDS

A Harmony Novel

Philip Gulley

HarperOne
A Division of HarperCollins Publishers

HarperOne

HarperCollins books may be purchased for educational, business, or sales promotional use. For information, please e-mail the Special Markets Department at SPsales@harpercollins.com.

HarperCollins Web site: http://www.harpercollins.com

HarperCollins®, 🌊®, and HarperOne™ are trademarks of HarperCollins Publishers.

FIRST HARPERCOLLINS PAPERBACK EDITION PUBLISHED IN 2007

Library of Congress Cataloging-in-Publication Data
Gulley, Philip.
Almost friends : a Harmony novel / Philip Gulley. — 1st ed.
p. cm.
ISBN: 978–0–06–089730–7
ISBN-10: 0–06–089730–9
1. City and town life—Fiction. 2. Quakers—Fiction. 3. Clergy—Fiction. 4. Harmony
(Ind.: Imaginary place)—Fiction. I. Title.
PS3557.U449A796 2006
813'.54—dc22   2005055065

17 RRD(H) 10 9 8 7 6 5

This novel is dedicated to Ray Stewart,
a friend of truth

Contents

How It All Started

For a one-legged man, Brother Lester the Evangelist was remarkably nimble, pacing back and forth across the front of the meeting room, stopping occasionally to pick up his Bible and wave it in the air like a sword, as if he were decapitating the infidels.

"You could be hit by a truck on your way home tonight," he bellowed. "You could be lying in your bed just as pretty as you please, and the Lord could raise up a tornado and knock your house flat." He paused for a moment, letting those horrific visions sink in. "You could be ate up with cancer and not even know it. Gone in the blink of an eye." He snapped his fingers. The sound reverberated across the room like a gunshot, causing Miriam Hodge, seated in the fourth row, to flinch.

"And don't think for a moment that your pretty clothes and your fancy homes and your college educations and big bank accounts will help you on the Day of Judgment. No siree, bob."

Bob Miles, jolted from slumber by the mention of his name, looked wildly about as Brother Lester continued. "Now is the day of decision. Right now, while you're still able."

Pastor Sam Gardner sat behind the pulpit, gripping the armrests of his chair, his eyes closed, praying fervently for Brother Lester to wind down. In lieu of that, he would settle for the meetinghouse to be flattened by a tornado; anything to bring Brother Lester's dreadful preachments to an end.

Sam's wife, Barbara, sat with their two sons in the fifth row, a glazed look on her face. This was the last night of the revival, and she'd begged to stay home. She'd only relented when Sam had reminded her that it was healing night, and Brother Lester had promised to make the lame walk and the blind see.

Regrettably, when a healing service is advertised in the newspaper, blind people are left out of the loop. Brother Lester took a stab at healing Asa Peacock of his nearsightedness, but apparently Asa's heart wasn't in it, and he left the healing service still wearing his glasses. Brother Lester had modest success healing Bea Majors's bunion. She skipped up and down the aisle and pronounced herself cured, but people had come expecting a more flamboyant miracle and were clearly disenchanted.

The revival concluded with a Sunday morning service. Brother Lester recounted the loss of his leg—a near escape involving cannibals in the heart of Africa. They'd gnawed his right calf down to the bone before he'd managed to get away. Gangrene had set in, and he'd lost his leg below his knee. His artificial leg was a bit short, causing him to list to the side.

Otherwise, Brother Lester was in fine form. He took a swipe at the Supreme Court, counseled the women to forsake pants, and said Hindus wouldn't be starving if they'd eat some of their cows. "The problem is, they think a cow might be their uncle in another life, and who wants to eat their uncle? Not me, that's for sure. So now they're starving, and their false religion is to blame."

Sam's head began to throb. What this had to do with the Christian faith, he wasn't sure.

Brother Lester paused from his sermonizing and cocked his head, as if listening to a voice only he could hear. "The Lord wants to know how come this church has a Furnace Committee and a Chicken Noodle Committee, but doesn't have an Evangelism Committee."

Dale Hinshaw, who had invited Brother Lester to revive them over the objections of the church's elders, reddened, clearly embarrassed at being affiliated with such indifferent believers, and even though it was a rhetorical question, he blurted out from the front row, "Tell the Lord it's not my fault. I've been telling 'em for years we need an Evangelism Committee. I even offered to head it up myself."

Brother Lester turned to glare at Sam. "Woe to the church that's lost its heart for helping the lost."

Sam was genuinely fond of the lost. It was the folks who were found who taxed his patience. He sat in his chair, his head resting in his hands, willing Brother Lester's rant to come to an end. He prayed for a bolt of lightning to strike Brother Lester. It wouldn't kill him. A man with a wooden leg is safely grounded, after all, an overlooked benefit of amputation. And as long as the Lord was throwing down lightning bolts, maybe He could singe Dale's eyebrows. That would set the two men back a notch or two. Sam smiled at the thought.

Fortunately, after a few pointed warnings about the fast-approaching apocalypse, Brother Lester took his seat next to Sam. They sat in silence. Sam studied him with sideways glances. Brother Lester was dressed to the nines, sporting a gold ring big enough to gag a camel. He was the kind of guy who preached about the end times, then took up an offering, which he invested in twenty-year bonds.

Sam sat quietly, thinking of Brother Lester, trying not to resent him. This frantic, hyper man with his private demons driving him from one place to another. Sam felt blessed that his brokenness was not quite as visible, that he was able to hide his imperfections—his nagging fears of worthlessness—under a veneer of religious duty.

Sam heard a rustle of noise, then the clearing of a throat. He looked up just as Dale Hinshaw rose to his feet to speak in the Quaker silence.

"I want to thank Brother Lester for coming here all the way from the deep jungles of Africa to bring us the Word. I think the Lord's anointed him mightily. I've said it before and I'll say it again, this church needs an Evangelism Committee, and I'm volunteering right here and now to be in charge of it, even if I got to do all the work myself."

He paused and looked around expectantly, as if hoping the congregation would burst into applause, then lift him on their shoulders and carry him to the pulpit, where they would lay hands on him, praising God for such a man.

"You do that, Dale," Fern Hampton called out. "Go right ahead."

That is how Dale Hinshaw was installed as the Chief Evangelist of Harmony Friends Meeting, unleashing a series of events not even the most clairvoyant among them could have anticipated, trials that would test Sam to the core and find him sadly lacking.

Two

Retirement and Other Frightful Matters

*I*t was a warm summer afternoon, and Sam Gardner was sitting in a lawn chair behind the Dairy Queen, eating an ice cream cone dipped in crunchies and visiting with Oscar Purdy.

"School bonds," Oscar said sagely. "Five percent a year, and you just sock it away. Forget it's there. That's the secret to retirement. How do you think me and Livinia got into that trailer park in Florida? School bonds, that's how."

"I have my retirement with the Quakers," Sam said. "I'll get about two hundred a month, plus my Social Security."

"You got a little nest egg set aside?" Oscar asked.

"I have some silver dollars my Grandpa gave me," Sam said. "And a coin collection. You know those quarters that have the different states on them? I got one of each of those."

"Thing is, you get those school bonds when you're young and you're set for life. Compound interest, that's the trick."

"And there's that rocking chair Barbara got from her grandmother," Sam said. "That's probably worth a little something."

"A fella can't start planning too early for retirement," Oscar said. "I bought my first bond when I was nineteen. Cost me one thousand dollars. Just kept plowing that money back into bonds and now that thousand dollars is worth eight thousand. Tax-free too. Won't have to pay Uncle Sam a dime."

Oscar leaned back in his chair, smiling at his immense good fortune. "Yep, it pays to start planning early. What's your plan, Sam?"

"I was kind of hoping the Lord would take care of me. Maybe lead some rich Dairy Queen owner who's invested in bonds to take pity on a poor servant of the Lord and help him out."

"Well, I tell you, Sam, wish I could help you out, but I'm a Methodist and feel I ought to help my own kind first. Hope you don't mind. Tell you what though, as long as I'm alive, I'll give you free crunchies on your cones. How's that?"

"Better than a sharp stick in the eye," Sam said.

The two men watched the traffic pass by on Highway 36 for a few minutes. Then Oscar, peering at the outside clock on the bank down the street, said, "Time was, a dog could take a nap in the middle of that road. Now the cars just whiz past. Seven in the past three minutes. Where do all these people come from?"

"Must be out-of-towners."

"If it keeps up, I might have to move," Oscar said. "Getting too hectic around here to suit me."

They watched the traffic a while longer. A fly buzzed around Sam's head, lured by the strawberry shampoo his wife bought by the gallon at Kivett's Five and Dime.

"Did I ever tell you my great-grandmother was a Quaker?" Oscar asked.

"No, you never mentioned that."

"Well, she was."

"I don't doubt it for a minute."

Oscar stretched in his chair and let out a contented sigh. "Yes, she surely was. But she married a Methodist and joined up with them, and that's how I ended up a Methodist."

"So if your Quaker great-grandmother hadn't consorted with a Methodist, you'd be a Quaker and I wouldn't have to worry about retirement?"

"That about sums it up," Oscar said.

"Isn't it funny, I mean, just think about it. Your great-grandmother falls in love with a man. Who knows why. She could just as easily have fallen in love with someone else. But she doesn't. She falls in love with a Methodist without giving any thought to how it might affect others. And as a result, here I am, a hundred years later, barely scraping by because the Dairy Queen tithe is going to the Methodists."

"Yeah, when you put it that way, it is kind of curious, isn't it?"

"That's my life story," Sam said wistfully. "Wrong place, wrong time."

"I'd have made a poor Quaker," Oscar said.

"You think?"

"Yeah, I'm not too sure about that pacifist stuff. I was in the Big War, you know."

"My secretary, Frank, went to war and he's a Quaker," Sam pointed out.

"But, growing up, he was a Baptist," Oscar said. "All his people were Baptist. He didn't become a Quaker till after the war."

"Tell you what, Oscar. If you become a Quaker, we'll waive the pacifist clause for you. And if a war comes along, you can go fight if you want. Just so long as you tithe."

"Too old to fight now. Besides, who'd run the Dairy Queen if I was off at war?"

"Well, you got me there."

"Not that I would shirk my patriotic duty, mind you. It's just that I have a responsibility here. People count on this place being open. They want an ice cream cone, and they expect me to be here to make them one. Why, if I weren't here, they'd have to drive all the way to Cartersburg on that narrow, twisty road to get one. Might even have a wreck and die, just because I was gone. No, my duty's here, Sam."

"I can see that now, Oscar."

Sam rose from his lawn chair and stretched. "Well, I'm off."

"Where you going?"

"Over to Grant's Hardware to look at the pocketknives."

"Good seeing you, Sam."

"Nice seeing you, Oscar. You take care now."

"Will do. And Sam, don't forget, school bonds."

"Got it," Sam said, tapping the side of his head.

In all the years Sam Gardner has lived in Harmony, he's never actually known anyone to retire, except for Miss Fishbeck, his sixth-grade teacher, who retired and moved to Las Vegas to help her sister, or so she said. It wasn't until after she left that people remembered she was an only child. They have no idea what she's up to out there but suspect she isn't teaching Sunday school.

People, of course, talk about retirement, then come up with a reason for avoiding it.

"My cousin, he retired after working forty-two years for the electric company, and his first day off he had a heart attack and fell over dead, just like that."

This is Harvey Muldock's unvarying excuse whenever his wife, Eunice, nags at him to turn their Plymouth dealership over to their children so she and Harvey can move to Florida for the winter.

"Your cousin weighed three hundred and fifty pounds and smoked like a chimney. He's lucky he made it that long," Eunice points out.

But Harvey isn't taking any chances.

If one is forced to retire, if he has no say in the matter, then he must volunteer to head up a committee at the church, fill an office at the Odd Fellows Lodge, or work part-time for Uly Grant at the hardware store. Staying home to watch TV is not an option, unless one has a thick hide and can endure the ridicule: "Must be nice to just sit around and do nothing. I wish I could do that. How do you get a job like that anyway?"

When Fern Hampton retired from teaching school, she took over the Friendly Women's Circle and has been running it ever since, even though Sam's mom had been elected president the past four years. Fern is intractable, an unyielding oak of a woman. Hit her with an ax, which Sam has been tempted to do many times, and it would bounce back and smack you in the head.

The right people never move to Las Vegas.

Once a month Fern marches into Sam's office and complains that the younger women in the church aren't pulling their weight. "They don't join the Circle. They don't make noodles. They barely show up for the Chicken Noodle Dinner."

"Most of them work in the daytime," Sam points out. "Maybe if you were to hold the meetings at night, more of them could come."

"The ladies don't like being out at night. You know that." To hear Fern tell it, Harmony after dark is inner-city Detroit. Murderers lurking on every corner, when mostly it's just Stanley Farlow taking his wife's poodle out for a tinkle.

The year before, Fern Hampton had urged the town board to sponsor a "Take Back the Streets Night," when everyone would leave their porch lights on and visit with their neighbors after dark. Fern had read about it in a magazine at the Kut 'n' Kurl. "That's what this town needs," she'd said. "Got to stand up to the criminal element." But taking back the streets implies someone has stolen them in the first place.

Nevertheless, the town board agreed, and everyone left their porch lights on, which gave some teenagers sufficient light to carry Fern Hampton's porch furniture up to her roof after she'd gone to bed. When word got out, there were letters to the *Herald,* written by people with short memories. People who, in their youth, had tipped over outhouses, smeared Limburger cheese on the radiators at the school, and emptied the town water tank onto Main Street. When the mayhem isn't their idea, they're dead set against it. But get them together at a class reunion and they'll chortle and snort at their misspent youth, when they did things that would get them jailed today.

Sam's church is full of these people, most of them useful citizens whom he genuinely loves. But a handful have caused him to study world religions, wondering if the grass might be greener on the other side of the theological fence. As far as he knows, the Buddhists don't have a Friendly Women's Circle. Or Dale Hinshaw.

He wanted to suggest to Fern that if she would retire from the Circle, it would open a slot for one of the younger women. But he held his tongue. Besides, Quakers seldom step aside. They have to be eased out or die. Fern has hinted that if they named the kitchen after her, she would retire from the Circle, but no one believes her. Her mother was the president of the Circle and in her dying words passed the legacy on to Fern. She made Fern promise she'd keep the presidency in the family. The only impediment to the Hampton dynasty is that Fern never married. She says she draws hope from the biblical story of Sarah, who bore a child at the age of ninety.

While Sam was at the library studying world religions, he saw Fern in the science section, over in the 500s, reading a book about artificial insemination. She'd once expressed the hope to Sam that God might miraculously impregnate her in order to continue the Hampton legacy, but God has not seen fit and no one's volunteered. Her hopes for a miracle dashed, she has now apparently turned to science.

Retirement and resignation are ways of letting go, something most people find difficult to do. So these Quakers labor on, some long after their usefulness, many to the point of annoyance. "Well, you do it however you want to," Fern tells the ladies whenever they float a new idea, and then proceeds to sabotage their every effort.

There is a fear of no longer being useful, of having people discover they can function without you. This appears to be Fern's deepest dread, that others won't find her indispensable. It is probably why she doesn't take vacations, for fear the church will run smoothly in her absence. So she is present for every event, directing, producing, and writing the script.

Along with his more generic anxieties, Sam fears a similar end, that one day his flock will discover they can live without him, that they will be swept off their feet by a newer, younger pastoral model and put Sam out to pasture. It is the fear of the middle-aged, that their careers will end before their retirement funds kick in, and they'll be forced to sell vacuum cleaners door to door. The press of years alarms Sam when he thinks about it, so he tries not to.

Avoidance of the inevitable is a popular pastime in Harmony. People in Sam's church talk in rosy tones about heaven and going to be with the Lord, but then fight it with all their might and seem shocked when death pays a visit.

"I saw him just last week, and he looked fine to me," Harvey Muldock told Stanley Farlow after Stanley's father, Russell, had died. Never mind that Russell Farlow was ninety-seven, had been in a nursing home for ten years, and was loaded with cancer. Harvey was still shocked. "What in the world happened?" he asked Stanley at the funeral.

People who can't imagine getting older and dying don't prepare for retirement. Oscar Purdy is the rare exception, and he didn't grow up here. He's a foreigner who moved to town from the city in 1946, after he and Livinia married. They met at a YMCA dance during the war. He was poor, but Livinia sensed he was destined for greatness, and her hunch was right. Between the Dairy Queen and his school bonds, he's worth a cool half a million. At least that's what Vernley Stout, over at the bank, reportedly said while under anesthesia at the dentist's office to have his wisdom teeth pulled.

Death. The shame of it. Not being useful to anyone but the undertaker. These are people who'll want to mow the clouds in heaven. Maybe suggest to the Lord that they form a committee to meet with the devil to discuss their mutual concerns in hopes of healing their historic division. Maybe form a softball league like they did with the Catholics, then go to the Dairy Queen afterwards. The Angels and the Imps eating their ice cream cones dipped in crunchies out back of the Dairy Queen with Oscar Purdy and Sam, discussing retirement and other frightful matters.

Three

The Light Shines in the Darkness

The following Sunday morning found Dale Hinshaw at the meetinghouse, agitated over what seemed to him to be Sam's clear departure from the gospel. It wasn't the first time he'd suspected Sam of sacrilege and likely wouldn't be the last. Sam had preached on evangelism that morning, suggesting that the gospel was best told with one's life, not one's lips.

The life-versus-lips controversy was not a new one at Harmony Friends Meeting. It had raged for years, popping up every couple months in one form or another. Dale came down on the lip side, while Sam was squarely in the life camp. Dale believed you had to tell people the gospel. It wasn't enough to live it. The hay had to be put down where the goats could get it. Then the goats needed to accept Jesus, *or else*.

The lips-versus-life battle erupted in the usual places, mostly during hymn selection. To Dale's great displeasure, Sam chose songs like "Take My Life and Let It Be," which Dale believed smacked of works-righteousness. He was a big fan of "I Love

to Tell the Story" and "We've a Story to Tell to the Nations."
Bea Majors, the organist and a fellow lips advocate, felt free to
change the hymns at the last minute if they didn't meet her
theological criteria. When Sam insisted they sing a works song,
she gave in, grudgingly, then warned the congregation not to
be seduced by the social gospel, which the liberals put forth
because they couldn't stand the rigors of true faith.

Over the years, Dale had taken careful notes on Sam's sermons, gathering evidence for the tribunal that would eventually charge Sam with heresy. His notes from today's sermon
were typical:

> Sam says living the Christian life is more important than
> talking about it. But see Romans 10:14 and Mark 13:10!!!
> Does Sam believe the gospel must be preached to all the
> nations or doesn't he??? If he does, then I will not stand
> against him, but if he doesn't, then I must shake the dust
> off my feet and leave this place!!! (See Matthew 10:14)
> Remind Sam that the harvest is plentiful but the laborers
> are few!!!! Talk to the elders about false prophets in the last
> days!!! (2 Peter 2:1) Is Sam a false prophet??? (See Deuter-
> onomy 13:1–5) If so, how should we kill him?

Dale tuned out Sam's sermon halfway through and began
writing a jingle for the Mighty Men of God evangelism contest, whose first prize was a month of free telephone Scripture greetings. Every household in the winner's locale would
be phoned every day and greeted with a Scripture that would

convict of them of their unrighteousness and bring them to repentance.

Dale was giddy at the thought of the entire town being hailed each day with a message from the Lord. He paused from his jingle writing to pray for God's guidance.

The jingle not only had to convict the depraved of their sin; it had to be short enough to fit on matchbooks, which could then be distributed in taverns across the nation, where the sinners set up shop.

Seated in the quiet, still smarting from Sam's sermon, Dale felt the fog lift from his mind and the perfect jingle descended, like a gift from above. Neatly penned underneath his reminder to kill Sam was a jingle he'd first thought of years before, when, inspired by Burma Shave ads, he'd erected signs throughout town calling his fellow Harmonians to the Lord.

> *Go to church and learn to pray,*
> *Or when you die, there's hell to pay.*

If that wouldn't bring saloon-goers to their knees, nothing would.

Dale went home and rifled through his past copies of the *Mighty Men of God* newsletter until he found the ad in the Easter edition of the newsletter. Though it was the Sabbath and he wasn't supposed to work, he knew the Lord would understand, these being the end times and all. He sat at his Corona typewriter and pecked out his jingle like a chicken grubbing for bugs. He folded it carefully, affixed an *In God We Trust* postage stamp to the envelope, walked it down to the post office, and deposited it in the mailbox, where Clarence, the mailman, would be sure to see it first thing in the morning.

Pleased by his faithful obedience to the Lord, Dale spent the rest of the day seated on his front porch surveying his latest marvel—a wooden windmill he'd constructed, which, when the blades turned, generated enough electricity to power a lightbulb at the top of the windmill. Underneath the lightbulb, he'd painted the words *Ye Are the Light of the World!* On windy nights, people from all over town drove past to see the blades spin and the light shine in the darkness.

Charles Gardner, Sam's father, had long maintained that Sunday was the one day when sitting around doing nothing didn't have to be excused. Indeed, sitting around doing nothing was a sign of one's commitment to the sixth commandment, "Remember the Sabbath Day, to keep it holy." The stores closed, even Kivett's Five and Dime, though Ned Kivett was not a churchgoer and hadn't been since the late 1970s, when the ladies of the Circle began buying the church's toilet paper from the Kroger, where it was eleven cents cheaper.

It's thirty years later, and Ned has still not forgiven them. Once a month he unloads on Sam. "All the years I've been a member of this church, teaching the high-school class and sponsoring a Little League team and setting up tables for the Chicken Noodle Dinner, and this is how you repay me? You people claim to be Christian, but I don't know. You think if St.

Peter had owned a Five and Dime, Jesus would have forsaken his friend to save a little money? You oughta be ashamed."

Ned was a tither, and the Five and Dime had prospered over the years. Whenever anyone moaned about the church's money problems, it was all Sam could do not to mention that the Circle's desire to save eleven cents had cost the church a hundred thousand dollars, some of which could have plumped up his salary. Instead, Ned wakes up early on Sundays, loads his pickup truck, and goes fishing at Raccoon Lake. Except in the winter, when he and his wife drive over to Cartersburg for the Sunday buffet at the Holiday Inn.

Sam would love a secular Sunday, but there was little chance of that. Even when he didn't speak, he was expected to be at church. The people who were most adamant about not working on Sundays never seemed to mind Sam working on Sundays.

He brought it up with his wife on their Sunday afternoon walk. "I tell you what drives me crazy. They not only work me like a borrowed mule; they're all the time saying how nice it must be to only have to work one day a week. Next time anyone says that to me, I'm gonna punch him in the nose."

They rounded the corner and walked down Main Street, past all the closed stores. "Am I the only one in this town who works on Sunday?"

"For crying out loud, Sam, you're a minister. Do you expect them to move worship to Thursdays, just so you can have a free weekend?"

"And what would be wrong with that? Most people get off work on Fridays and have the whole weekend ahead of them to enjoy. I have to spend Saturdays getting ready for Sunday, then spend Sunday at church."

"You get Mondays off," Barbara pointed out.

"Unless someone is in the hospital or has an emergency or wants me to do something, which is just about every week."

"Sam Gardner, you are so cynical. Why can't you be more positive?"

"I've been talking with the other ministers. We're thinking of going on strike until they move worship to a different day," Sam said.

"You mean have a different day be the Sabbath?"

"That's right."

"Then the new day would be the Sabbath and you'd still have to work."

Sam paused for a moment, then frowned. "Well, I guess we hadn't thought about that."

"You have some real Einsteins in that ministerial association," Barbara laughed.

"What I need," Sam announced, "is a sabbatical. They're supposed to give you one every seven years. I've been doing this eighteen years without hardly a break. Eighteen years!"

Barbara reached over and took his hand. Her voice softened. "Why not ask them for some time off, honey. You could spend time with your Dad. You're always saying you don't see him enough. And he's getting older. He won't be around forever. Maybe you could take a little vacation with him. Go visit some hardware stores or whatever it is you men like to do. Maybe even take the boys with you. They'll be off to college before you know it."

"Wouldn't work," Sam said. "They'd never let me off. And if they did, they wouldn't pay me. Can't afford to take time off without pay."

"Maybe I could get a temporary job. Deena's told me I could come work full-time at the Legal Grounds anytime I wanted."

"Nah, I'll be all right. You know me, I just like having something to moan about."

They ambled past Dale Hinshaw's house. Dale waved to them from the front porch.

"Don't stop," Sam whispered.

"Hey, Sam. You're just the man I needed to see."

"I can't go anywhere," Sam muttered under his breath.

Barbara spoke to Dale. "Perhaps it could wait until Tuesday. Sam's off the clock right now."

Dale went on, oblivious. "I've been thinking about this Evangelism Committee we've got going, and I think it's time we got a little more serious about things. I got this idea I want to tell you about."

"Not today, Dale," Barbara said. "No more work for Sam today. And tomorrow's his day off. But he'd be happy to talk with you on Tuesday."

A pouty look crossed Dale's face. "One of these one-hour-a-week Christians, eh?"

"He'll see you on Tuesday," Barbara told Dale, taking Sam by the elbow and steering him down the sidewalk. "There are days I'd like to choke that man," she muttered, when they were out of earshot.

Sam figured every member of every Harmony Friends Meeting had entertained the notion of choking Dale Hinshaw at one time or another.

They turned the corner and approached Sam's parents' home.

"It looks like they're taking a nap," Barbara observed.

"Let's wake them up."

They walked up the sidewalk and clomped hard up the wooden stairs to the porch. His parents stirred to life. His father stood and stretched, then sat back down on the swing, sliding over to make room for Sam and Barbara.

"Beautiful day, isn't it?" Gloria Gardner noted.

"It certainly is," Sam agreed.

"I'm glad you came by," his mother said. "I was talking with Fern this morning about fixing up the nursery, and we wanted to know if you could help us paint tomorrow."

"Tomorrow's his day off," Barbara said.

"It's not like it's church work. It's more like helping your mother. Your father would do it, but he's been having these bad headaches lately, and the paint fumes make it worse."

"Feels like someone is just peeling the skin right off my head," Sam's dad blurted out. He had a way of describing his headaches that gave everyone else a headache. "It's like they've sawed right through my skull and started beating my brain with a hammer. Man, it hurts."

"I get the picture," Sam said. "Can we change the subject?"

"So can you help your poor, saintly mother tomorrow?" his mom asked again.

"Well, it was my day off ..." Sam said.

"Day off! What the heck you need a day off for? You only work one day a week as it is. Boy, I wish I had a job like that," his dad said, then adjusted his pants, which were riding up, stretched one more time, closed his eyes, and resumed his Sabbath slumber.

four

Krista's Dream

Some people come kicking and screaming to ministry; others seem born for it, slipping into it as easily as a hand slides into a silken glove. For as long as she could remember, Krista Riley had wanted to be a priest, and although her parents had always told her she could be anything she wanted, they apparently hadn't counted on the pope's inflexibility on that particular matter.

As a child she would sit and watch the priest holding the host aloft, his face radiant, and she longed to do what he did. The church's only concession was to let her be an altar girl, which placed her in the vicinity of the altar, but not close enough to satisfy; it was like sitting on the sidelines and never getting to play.

The week she turned thirteen, her grandfather died in their living room, on the hospital bed they'd rented from the drugstore. She'd spent the day holding her grandpa's hand, wondering how many other people had rented this bed to die on. Everyone else had drifted in and out of the room, uneasy with death, but she had stayed by his side, strangely at ease, every now and then patting his hand and wiping his brow. By the time the priest had arrived to anoint her grandpa's pale head and pray for him, Krista knew God had called her to the ministry, just as surely as if Jesus had appeared in the room, pointed an elegant finger at her, and said, "Follow thou me."

"I want to be a priest," she'd told her mother that night.

"You can't. You're a girl. They don't allow women to be priests."

"You've always told me I can be anything I want."

There is a tendency among the young and idealistic to believe if people are simply presented with the facts, they will make a reasonable decision. "I've been thinking," Krista told her mother later that evening, "and unless there's something you haven't told me, the big difference between men and women is that men have a ... well, you know ... and we don't."

Her mother blushed.

"I know all about it," Krista went on. "They told us about it in health class. They have one and we don't and that's the big difference. Right?"

"There are others, of course, but I'd say that's the more obvious one," her mother admitted.

"So, practically speaking, there's no good reason to keep a woman from being a priest?"

"That's right, dear. Though I think it's written in the Bible that women can't be priests."

It took Krista two days to find the verse her mother had mentioned, but it was there, in Paul's first letter to Timothy, chapter 2, verse 12: "I permit no woman to teach or to have authority over men; she is to keep silent."

A careful reading of the verse indicated that, although the Apostle Paul permitted no woman to teach, God's opinion of women leaders was left unstated. When she pointed this out to her mother, her mother said, "I think they believe the Apostle Paul is speaking for God."

"But how can they be sure? Isn't it dangerous to assume someone else is always speaking for God?"

Her mother sighed, then rubbed her temples. "Krista, honey, I love you to death. But these questions of yours give me a headache. Tell you what, honey, why don't you write our priest a letter and ask him these things?"

But Krista had always been told to go to the top, so she wrote the pope instead.

It was amazingly simple. She wrote the letter on unlined paper, in neat rows and tidy script, expressing her desire to be a priest and wanting to know if the pope might make an exception in her case. "Though I don't have everything a man has"—she thought he'd know what she meant, so she didn't elaborate—"I do love God and believe I'm called to spend my life serving Him." She studied the word *Him*. She didn't for a moment believe God was a Him, but she let it stand, just so the pope wouldn't think she was a radical out to make a point.

Then she rode her bicycle to the post office, where they gave her the address for the Vatican, which she carefully copied onto the envelope, before sealing it closed and sliding it down the chute into the bin of stamped mail.

While she waited to hear back from the pope, she practiced being a priest. She conducted three funerals for neighborhood pets and visited Mrs. Harvey, down the street, who'd broken her ankle while carrying in the groceries.

Though Mrs. Harvey had never married and was technically not a Mrs., it seemed odd to call a woman of her age "Miss." Krista, in addition to being taught she could be anything she wanted and to always go to the top, had also been advised to call adults Mr. or Mrs. Though Mrs. Harvey had a heavy mustache, she was clearly a woman in other respects.

Like Krista, Mrs. Harvey was Catholic, and when Krista told her about wanting to be a priest, the ponderous woman flopped back in her recliner and rolled her eyes heavenward, her many chins quivering in alarm. "You can't be a priest. They don't allow it."

"How come?"

"Because you're a girl."

"Could you please explain why that should make a difference?"

Mrs. Harvey frowned. "Should the church change its mind and allow women to be priests, you need to keep something in mind."

"What's that?"

"It's impolite to visit someone in their home under the pretense of consoling them, and then argue religion with them."

Krista thought for a moment. "Yes, I suppose you're right. I'm sorry. How is your ankle?"

"Not well at all. The doctor thinks he might have to operate."

"Would you like me to pray for you?"

"Yes, I suppose there'd be no harm in that."

Krista laid her hand on Mrs. Harvey's bruised and swollen ankle. "Dear Lord, thank you for Mrs. Harvey and the gift of her life. Please grant her peace in these arduous days and, if it be your will, heal her ankle. Amen."

Krista seldom used words like *grant* and *arduous,* but they seemed fitting words for a prayer and, besides, it never hurt to expand one's vocabulary.

"Thank you, Krista. That was a lovely prayer. I feel better already." Mrs. Harvey leaned back in her recliner with a contented sigh and closed her eyes.

Krista looked around the room. Beams of sunlight were blazing through the window, lighting up the dust motes. In the next room, Mrs. Harvey's dog napped under the dining room table, his rib cage rising and falling with a wiffling snore, his whitened muzzle occasionally twitching to the rhythm of a canine dream.

"How old is your dog?" Krista asked.

"Fourteen."

Krista thought for a moment, calculating figures in her head, then said, "That's ninety-eight in dog years. If he dies anytime soon, I'll be happy to do his funeral."

"Thank you, Krista."

"It wouldn't be my first funeral. I've done three so far. Two cats and a squirrel."

"Who had a squirrel?"

"I'm not certain who he belonged to. I found him on the road in front of our house. He was starting to stink, so I had to bury him quick."

"That was very kind of you," Mrs. Harvey said. "The animals are God's children too."

"Is there anything else I can do for you?"

"No, thank you. I'll be fine."

"If you had a husband, he could help you," Krista pointed out. "Why didn't you ever marry?"

Mrs. Harvey opened her eyes and heaved herself forward in the recliner. "It's impolite to ask questions about one's marital status. People might think you're a gossip, and no one likes a gossip."

"I was just wondering."

"Ministers must be discreet. That means you don't ask people personal questions unless they volunteer the information."

"People ask me personal questions all the time."

"You are under no obligation to answer them," Mrs. Harvey said. "Why do people think every question must be answered? When I was a child, people knew to mind their own business."

"I think I'll be going now," Krista said. "Thank you for letting me visit you."

"What have you learned today?"

"I learned not to argue theology with people in their homes, that prayer makes you feel better, not to ask personal questions, that no one likes a gossip, that ministers should be discreet, and not to answer a question just because someone asks it."

"Very good, Krista. Come back tomorrow and I'll teach you more."

"Okay, I'll see you then."

But her best friend's hamster died the next day, so Krista spent the day making funeral arrangements and cheering her friend in her time of loss. It was well after supper before she'd remembered her promise to visit Mrs. Harvey, and by then it was too late. She had the distinct feeling that one of Mrs. Harvey's rules for clergy concerned the proper hours for visitation.

If she was going to be a priest, she would have to learn to keep better track of her time.

A month passed before she heard back from the Vatican. The letter was in Latin, which she asked her priest to translate. He did, but grew distressed when he discovered one of his parishioners had gone over his head to the pope. "There's a rule for things like this," he told her. "First, you ask your parents, and if they can't help you, you ask me. If I don't know the answer, we go to the bishop, and if he doesn't know, we go to the cardinal. You don't start out with the pope. Now what is it you wanted to know?"

"I think God is calling me to be a priest," Krista said.

"Impossible," the priest said. "God doesn't call women to be priests. It's against the rules. You think God is going to break His own rules?"

"How do we know that's God's rule?"

"We just know, that's how."

"Did God tell you that was His rule?"

"A long time ago, many hundreds of years, God told the pope. Then the pope told the cardinals, the cardinals told the bishops, the bishops told the priests, and we told the people."

"I know that game," Krista said. "We played it once at school. The teacher whispered something in my ear, and I whispered it to someone else, and it went all around the room. Anyway, by the time it got back to the teacher, it wasn't anything close to what she'd told me. Maybe God told the pope He wanted women to be priests, but by the time it got to us, it was all mixed up."

"That doesn't happen in the church," the priest said, a hint of exasperation creeping into his voice. "God protects His church from error."

"What about Galileo?"

"What about Galileo?" the priest asked.

"The church told Galileo he was wrong, but he turned out to be right, which means the church was wrong."

"Who told you that?"

"My catechism teacher, Sister Therese."

"Well, there you go," the priest said, changing the subject. "You could be a nun like Sister Therese."

"I don't want to be a nun. I want to be a priest. Sister Therese doesn't want to be a nun anymore either. She wants to be a priest. She told me so herself."

The priest mumbled something about relocating Sister Therese to another parish.

For as long as she lived at home, Krista was determined to be a priest, but the church stood firm. So she went to college and became a teacher, and though it was gratifying work, it wasn't enough, like ordering chocolate ice cream and having to settle for vanilla. It was good, but it wasn't her first choice.

Even though Krista was not married, the children in her class addressed her as Mrs. Riley. When she turned thirty she stopped correcting them. Occasionally, one of her students would ask her why she didn't have a husband.

"It's impolite to ask questions about one's marital status. People might think you're a gossip, and no one likes a gossip," she would tell them.

But it didn't keep them from wondering.

With nuns in scarce supply, she taught the catechism classes at church. But every Sunday, she longed to stand where the priest stood, elevating the host and reciting the beautiful cadence of the Mass. But no one moves as slowly as those who hoard God's blessings for themselves, so year after year she sat and watched and kept her calling to herself, lest the ire of fearful souls kill it off.

Charlie Gardner's Confession

C harlie Gardner was lying in bed when he had his first
heart attack. At least he thought it was a heart attack.
The week before he'd read the symptoms while waiting at the Rexall for Thad Cramer to fill his prescription.
Thad had posted the symptoms of major diseases on the wall
of the pharmacy. Charlie, who dabbled in hypochondria, read
them and grew alarmed, convinced he was suffering some
dreadful malady. He had come home one day worried he was
entering menopause.

Lying in bed, he tried to recall the signs of a heart attack—a
heavy weight in the chest, numbness in the arms, sweating,
and difficulty breathing.

He thought of waking his wife, but decided against it.
She'd want to call Johnny Mackey to come with his ambulance. He'd have to go to the hospital in Cartersburg, instead
of going fishing with Asa Peacock the next morning, as he
had planned. So, being a fatalist, he decided that if this were

the time and manner in which the Lord had deemed to take him, who was he to resist God's will?

Charlie lay perfectly still, asking forgiveness for specific sins he'd committed. Then, just to cover his bases, he sought forgiveness for his inadvertent sins, wanting to go out with a clean slate. Years ago, back in the 1960s, on a trip to the city, he'd bought a girlie magazine. He had hidden it out in the garage, in the cabinet underneath his drill press. He resolved to throw it away if he lived to see the sun rise.

He grew alarmed thinking of the magazine. What if he died and his wife and minister son found it while going through his things? What would they think of him? He probably couldn't have his funeral in the church after that. They'd have to bury him in the pagan section of the cemetery, along with the town ne'er-do-wells.

After a while, whatever was sitting on his chest rose and left, and he began to feel better, so he got out of bed and went out to the garage to throw the magazine in the trash. He buried it deep in the garbage can, underneath the coffee grounds.

When Charlie came out of the garage, his wife was standing in the kitchen doorway.

"What are you doing up?"

Charlie had never been quick on his feet; he paused while he contemplated how to answer.

"Uh, there's something about me you don't know."

Gloria Gardner looked at him the way she looks at him when she doesn't believe what he's about to say. "And what would that be?"

"I've got a drinking problem."

A drinking problem was infinitely safer than a *Playboy* problem, the former being a disease beyond his control, the latter being a moral failure that could get him divorced, or killed.

"A drinking problem? You mean you're an alcoholic?"

Charlie feigned embarrassment. "'Fraid so."

"And how long have you had this drinking problem?"

"All my life I guess," Charlie explained. "It's not like I can help it. It's a disease, you know."

"I've never subscribed to that notion," Gloria Gardner said. "If it were a disease, people couldn't stop. People stop drinking every day. I think it's a moral issue."

This wasn't going as well as Charlie had hoped.

"Let me smell your breath," she commanded.

He exhaled on her.

"Just as I suspected. I don't smell a thing."

"That's because I've been drinking vodka. You think I'm stupid enough to drink something people could smell?"

Charlie walked into the house, brushing past her, perturbed. "It's a terrible thing when a husband tells his wife he's a drunk and she doesn't believe him. You ought to be ashamed of yourself."

Gloria went out to the garage and poked around, looking behind the mower and in his workbench drawers, but couldn't find anything. When she came back in their bedroom, he was sprawled across their bed, clutching his chest.

"Now what's wrong?"

"I think I'm having a heart attack."

"Oh, sure. Try to get out of trouble by faking a heart attack. You think I'd fall for that old trick?"

That's the problem with dishonesty—one lie casts doubt on a thousand truths.

He lay in bed thinking of his death. It was what he'd always hoped for whenever the subject of death arose—to die in bed, at home, next to his wife. To just not wake up. Somehow, though, it was more difficult than he'd imagined. For instance, getting someone to believe he was dying wasn't as easy as he'd thought.

He rolled over, grabbed the phone, and dialed Sam's house. It rang three times before his son answered.

"Hi, Sam."

"Hey, Dad."

"I'm having a heart attack."

"What? Are you sure?"

"Pain in the chest, my arm hurts. Yep, I'm pretty sure."

"Is Mom there?" Sam asked, starting to sound frantic.

"Yeah, she's right here. Do you want to talk with her?"

"Yes."

Sam's mother came on the line.

"I'll be right over," Sam told her. "Meanwhile, I want you to call Johnny Mackey to come with the ambulance."

"Oh, he's fine. I caught him out in the garage doing something and he's trying to drum up sympathy. I can't believe he called and woke you and Barbara up. Go back to bed."

And with that she hung up the phone.

"It'd serve you right if I died," Charlie groaned from his side of their bed.

But his wife was already fast asleep. That woman could sleep standing up.

He lay still, making his peace with death. He thought that perhaps it was better this way—to die in the peace and quiet of his own home, instead of at the hospital among strangers poking him full of needles.

The birds woke him a little before eight. He looked around, surprised that heaven looked so much like his old bedroom. Then he smelled coffee in the kitchen. He got up, went to the bathroom, pulled on his bathrobe, and tromped downstairs to the kitchen.

"Why didn't you wake me up?" he groused. "I was supposed to go fishing with Asa Peacock."

"I thought since you'd had a heart attack, you might need the extra sleep," Gloria said.

It was embarrassing to be on the verge of death, then to recover as wholly and quickly as he had. It caused people to doubt your sincerity.

"Since you're not going fishing, maybe you could mow the lawn today," she went on. "It's looking pretty shabby. And don't forget to take out the trash. It's starting to smell."

She walked over and kissed the top of his balding head. "I'm glad you didn't die."

That made it a little easier.

"Want some pancakes?" she asked.

"Sure."

He ate four of them. He was famished. Almost dying could wear a man out.

Sam stopped by his parents' house on his way to work. Walking over, he'd decided not to bring up the night before. Who knew what went on between two married people, after all. It seemed the wiser course to avoid the topic altogether. But his father wouldn't let it rest.

"Your mother tried to kill me last night," he announced, between bites of pancake. "I was having a heart attack and I called you to come get me, but she hung up the phone. I think she's after my life insurance money."

"If he's having a heart attack, ask him why he felt good enough to be sneaking around out in the garage at three o'clock in the morning."

When Sam was a child, his parents had presented a united front against their children. If they had their differences, they settled them privately, out of earshot. Now that their sons were raised, they felt free to turn on one another and enlist Sam on one side or the other.

"By the way," his mother said. "Your father has a drinking problem."

"No, I don't."

"You said so yourself last night."

"I was just kidding. Can't you take a joke?" He turned to Sam. "She never could take a joke."

"Then what were you doing out in the garage?"

Charlie sighed, then appeared hurt. "If you must know, I was checking on your anniversary present."

Their anniversary was the following week, which he hadn't remembered until that morning when he'd noticed it written on the refrigerator calendar.

"You remembered our anniversary?"

"Of course I did."

Gloria bent down to kiss his head. "You're a regular Clark Gable."

Charlie tilted his head for another kiss.

Sam wasn't sure what was worse—watching his parents fight or kiss. He glanced at his watch. "Would you look at the time? I gotta go. I'll see you later."

His parents were too distracted to see him to the door.

Charlie Gardner had painted himself in the corner with his mention of an anniversary gift. Now his wife had her hopes up, and an ordinary gift wouldn't do. At the very least, this meant a trip to the Wal-Mart in Cartersburg. She'd been hinting around for a television set for the kitchen so she could watch the *Today Show* while she drank her morning coffee. It had caused an argument when she'd first suggested it.

"What, aren't I good enough to talk to anymore?" he'd asked her. "You don't even know those people. They sit up there in New York City in their fancy high-rise apartments and limousines, and you'd rather spend your morning with them than with me. That's a fine how-do-you-do after all the years we've been married."

"You know that's not true."

"Then why didn't we go to Florida last winter? You don't want to be alone with me, that's why."

Charlie brings up their almost trip to Florida every time they argue. Winter depresses him, so this past December he'd suggested they spend a few months in Florida, at his cousin's condo south of Tampa. But Gloria had nixed the idea and suggested he take an antidepressant instead.

"Oh, you'd like that, wouldn't you? Get me all drugged up and have me declared incompetent, then take all the money."

"Money?" she'd asked. "What money? Where's all this money you're talking about?"

"Are you saying I haven't taken good care of you? Is that what you're saying?"

They didn't speak to each other for several hours before making up. Arguments for them are a slow-release aphrodisiac. They start their day bickering, then by afternoon are steaming up the windows.

Charlie drove to Cartersburg that afternoon and bought a television set small enough to sit on their kitchen countertop. Gloria watched him unload it from the car and carry it into the garage. When he walked in the door, she asked, "What was that you were carrying in?"

"You shouldn't be so nosy around our anniversary."

"I thought my anniversary gift was already out there. Isn't that what you told Sam this morning?"

"You think that's all I got you?" Charlie asked. "For crying out loud, can't a guy get his wife two presents?"

It was turning out to be an expensive anniversary.

Under the guise of visiting Dr. Neely to have his heart checked, Charlie drove to Kivett's Five and Dime and bought Gloria a parakeet. They'd had a dog, Zipper, for years, but she had died the month before, which had not been soon enough. In her last year the dog had taken to rolling in road-kill, then barging indoors to snooze behind the couch, where she couldn't be dislodged.

On the upside, having Zipper provided an excuse not to visit certain relatives on his wife's side of the family. When she had suggested visiting her sister in Minnesota, he'd said, "Who's going to take care of Zipper? Were you just going to leave her here and let her starve to death? Is that what you want? You never did like our dog, did you?"

But with the dog dead, Charlie was without an excuse for staying home, so he bought his wife a parakeet so that he could continue avoiding people who annoyed him.

He used to worry they would divorce, but now the momentum of years is on their side. Charlie attributes their longevity to arguments. He believes couples who talk out their problems are eventually exhausted by dialogue and find it easier to part company, while arguing permits a couple to settle disagreements with a quick, loud efficiency. At least this is his theory, and so far he's been right.

As for not going to bed mad, if they did that, they'd never sleep. Fortunately, Charlie and Gloria are blessed with short memories and wake up in love. The very passion that drives them to argue is the same passion that gets Charlie pumped and primed when he catches a glimpse of his wife's naked collarbone. Then they're off to the races. Ardor, they have learned in their almost fifty years, is a welder's heat, cleaving them one day, joining them together the next.

Six

The Chief Evangelist

*I*n the one month since Dale Hinshaw had proclaimed himself the Chief Evangelist of Harmony Friends Meeting, he'd managed to alienate half the congregation. Attendance at worship had declined precipitously, owing to Dale's weekly rants about people not coming to church. Why he scolded the people who did show up was a mystery to everyone.

Attendance always declined in the summer, due to vacations and family reunions. But every year it was the same; Sam panicked through July, until Barbara reminded him folks would return in the fall, refreshed and rarin' to go, just when Sam was pooped and in need of time off.

Dale Hinshaw, who kept careful records of who was attending and who wasn't, didn't help matters. "The Muldocks were gone today," he announced to Sam at the front door after worship one Sunday. "Asa told me they were going to the Methodist church now. Ellis and Miriam weren't here last Sunday or today. Plus, the Iversons haven't been here for a month."

"The Muldocks are at the Methodist church today because Harvey's niece is having her baby baptized. Ellis and Miriam are on vacation in Michigan, and the Iversons went back east to visit their parents," Sam explained.

Even though he had perfectly plausible explanations, Sam felt a rumble of anxiety deep in his bowels.

"I saw the Iversons yesterday at the Dairy Queen," Dale said. "They're back in town. I wonder why they weren't here?"

"Maybe they just wanted to spend a quiet morning at home. Maybe they went to the state park for the day to have a picnic. Maybe they got tired of certain people badgering them about why they hadn't been to church."

Subtlety is lost on Dale. So too, for that matter, is the obvious. "I think I'll give them a call," he said, then paused. "No, I think we ought to go see them in person. When can you go?"

"I'm not going anywhere," Sam said firmly.

"I think you've forgotten our Lord's counsel that two should go to confront a brother who's lost in sin."

"Who said the Iversons are lost in sin? They've been visiting with family. They go every summer when Paul gets out of school. Wanting to see your aging parents is not a sin."

"Let the dead bury the dead, that's what I say," Dale intoned piously. Then he pulled a computer printout from the inside pocket of his plaid sport coat. "I did a graph on our attendance. As you can see, we're down 28 percent in the past month. It appears the Lord has turned His back on us."

Dale had purchased a computer that spring and had pestered Sam ever since, presenting him with pie charts and bar graphs chronicling their church's decline. "The way I got it figured, we'll have to close the doors next February if we don't do something right now."

Tossing Dale out of the church would reverse the decline, but Sam was too charitable to say so.

Of course, Dale has been predicting their church's demise ever since he began attending decades ago. The computer has only allowed him to do it more dramatically. He bombards people with e-mails, calling down the wrath of God on those who won't forward his missives along. Apparently too cheap to buy virus protection, he has infected half the computers in town, causing them to crash and their owners to long for his slow and torturous death.

"I could always e-mail the Iversons," Dale said. "I got this story I've been wanting to send them anyway."

Dale's e-mail stories invariably concerned themselves with tales of people who'd slighted the Lord, causing all manner of misfortune to befall them.

"Let's give them another week," Sam suggested.

"Well, just so you know their souls are in your hands, not mine. I tried to get 'em right with the Lord. It won't be my fault if they die this week and go to hell."

"I'll assume all responsibility," Sam assured Dale.

Talking with Dale reminded Sam what he dreaded about his job—facing Dale Hinshaw after worship. It never failed. When Sam uttered the final amen, Dale could be depended upon to make a beeline for him, generally to critique his sermon. Over the years, Sam had become adept at smiling while Dale prattled on, pretending to listen while thinking of his afternoon nap.

Indeed, that was what he was doing that very moment, when Dale's question brought him back to the present.

"...and so that's what I was gonna do. What do you think, Sam?"

"I think it's a wonderful idea, Dale."

Sam had no idea what wacky scheme he'd just endorsed, but was too tired to care.

"So you don't mind, then?"

"Not at all. Best of luck to you," Sam said, then turned to greet Bea Majors. "What a Sunday morning! Bea, I don't know how you make that organ sound the way you do."

Bea made the organ sound like a catfight, so Sam was purposely vague with his comments, which allowed him to retain his integrity, while Bea, like most people who have an inflated regard for their talent, thought him sincere.

He shook hands and visited with his flock for another ten minutes, before gathering his Bible and sermon notes from the pulpit, turning off the lights, and locking the doors.

Locking the doors is something new for Sam. The doors of the meetinghouse have been unlocked since 1949, when Harry Darnell, who headed the trustees, bolted to the Methodist church in a huff and took the key to the church with him.

No one noticed it missing until 1972, when a vanload of hippies driving through town stopped for the night and slept on the pews. When Pastor Taylor discovered them the next morning, they were seated cross-legged around the pulpit in the midst of transcendental meditation. He phoned the police, who came and arrested them, even though the door was unlocked and a sign on the door said, "All are welcome." The transcendental meditation was the hippies' undoing. If they'd been saying the Lord's Prayer, Pastor Taylor would have fallen to his knees and joined them.

It led to the first church fight Sam remembers. The next Sunday, Ellis Hodge had casually suggested they put a new lock on the church door, which had caused Dale Hinshaw to achieve orbit. "Yes, and just as soon as we do that, somebody might want to come inside and get saved and he'll be locked out. Do you want that on your conscience? I sure don't!"

"Why can't folks get themselves saved on the front steps?" Ellis had asked.

A perfectly reasonable question, it triggered a half-hour harangue from Dale Hinshaw on the importance of accepting the Lord at altars. "I think you've clearly forgotten Scripture's reminder that the Lord is in His holy temple. It doesn't say the Lord is on the front steps of the temple. It says He's in the temple."

"Isn't that in the Old Testament?" Ellis had asked. "What's that got to do with us?"

"Are you saying the Lord's a liar?" Dale had screeched. "If He said it then, He means it now. No ifs, ands, or buts."

This had led to an hour-long argument on whether or not Christians were obligated to follow the Old Testament.

The battle wounds cut so deep it had taken decades to get a lock put on. Even then, someone had to sneak and do it, and that person had not confessed. Dale Hinshaw has been looking for the culprit ever since. The month before, Sam had come to meeting and there it was, a brand-new lock on the church door with three keys taped to it. He's been locking it ever since, except when he forgets, which happens more often than he'd like to admit.

Dale suspects Ellis Hodge is the guilty party and has tried to wring a confession from him, but Ellis won't budge, so Dale has been looking to bring him up on other charges, with little success.

Sam doesn't spend a lot of time reflecting on these matters for fear it will cause him to leave the ministry. Sometimes his father will recall a particularly grisly episode in the church's history, and Sam will have to leave the room so as not to become too discouraged at the prospect of pastoring such malcontents as Dale Hinshaw.

In his first five years at Harmony, Sam had made every effort to steer Dale in the right direction. He tried reasoning with Dale, directing Dale's vast energies down more reasonable paths. It never worked. Now Sam was trying a different approach, one that involved the total abdication of pastoral responsibility—letting Dale do whatever he pleased, which was what Dale generally did anyway.

As they walked home from meeting, Barbara said, "I saw you talking with Dale. What's he want to do now?"

"I don't know," Sam said. "I wasn't paying attention."

"Doesn't that worry you?"

"I'm sure whatever Dale does, it'll work out fine," Sam said.

Barbara studied him for a moment. "Are you feeling all right? Have you hit your head and didn't tell me? Because what you just said suggests you might be suffering from a brain defect." She touched his forehead. "You don't feel fevered."

"I've just decided I've spent too much time worrying about Dale Hinshaw. At some point I'm going to have to relax and trust the Lord."

"Trusting the Lord sounds nice in theory," Barbara said. "It's what all the martyrs said just before they were killed."

Sam elected not to respond.

Their sons had run on ahead, so it was just the two of them. They rounded the corner by the Legal Grounds Coffee Shop, walked past the *Harmony Herald* office, then paused to look in the window of Grant's Hardware. A sign was taped to the glass. *For Rent. Apartment Above Hardware Store. No pets, smoking, alcohol, rock music, or loud parties allowed.*

"I guess Uly fixed up Kenny Hutchens's old room," Sam said.

"Who's Kenny Hutchens?"

"He mowed lawns and hauled trash when I was a kid. Uly's dad rented him the room upstairs, but no one's lived there since Kenny died. That was years ago. Back in the 1970s, at least. I wonder what it looks like up there now?"

Barbara shuddered. "I'd hate to think."

"Maybe I should rent it," Sam mused. For the past several years, since his sons had begun bickering as if it were an Olympic sport, Sam had dreamed of having a quiet retreat. Initially, he'd thought of buying a cabin in the woods outside of town. But desperation had made him less picky, and the room over Grant's Hardware seemed more than sufficient.

"You keep wanting to get away from us," Barbara said. "What's wrong with our house?"

"Nothing at all. I just thought it'd be nice to have a little place I could slip away to and read. Someplace without a phone, where I could have a little peace and quiet."

"Peace and quiet? Why do men always need peace and quiet? Boy, it's a good thing we women didn't always need to go away for a little peace and quiet or nothing would get done."

Sam chuckled and draped his arm across his wife's shoulders. "Women are the stronger sex. No doubt about it. But if you must know, I wanted the peace and quiet to write a book."

"A book? You hate writing," Barbara pointed out. "When you have to write your article for the church newsletter, you complain about it for days on end."

"That's different. I have to write that. If I wrote a book, I could write what I wanted."

"I'm the one who should write a book," Barbara said. "I've got things I've been wanting to get off my chest for years."

Sam was feeling frisky—like his father, squabbling excited him—and he thought dreamily of his wife's chest. He took her hand. "I have an idea," he said. "Why don't we rent Uly's apartment and not tell the boys where we've moved. Then we'll both have peace and quiet!"

They walked another block without speaking. Sam was thinking of peace and quiet and how dear it has become to him. He used to have a high tolerance for chaos and clatter. When the boys were younger and would quarrel, he would reason with them, trying to understand how their fight had begun. Now he doesn't care who started it; all he wants is for their sons to hit one another quietly.

Sam feels the same way about church. He has given up illusions of pastoring a megachurch. Now he just wishes people would get along. Being a pastor is like negotiating a minefield—one wrong step and your world explodes, so you tread carefully. Like the month before when Frank had suggested they ask the trustees to put a new lock on the front door of the meetinghouse. Sam had advised against it. "You don't want to go there," he'd told his secretary. "Because Dale Hinshaw will want to rehash everything. It's better just to leave it alone."

When Sam had come to work the next morning, the new lock was on the door and Frank was putting away his tools.

"I know nothing," Sam said. "I saw nothing. I heard nothing. I have no idea where that new lock came from."

"What new lock?" Frank asked.

There are some things it's best not to know—which of your children started the fight, why it took fifty years to replace a lock, or what grand scheme Dale Hinshaw might be cooking up. Knowledge is a good thing, but ignorance is not to be discounted.

Seven

Krista's Big Plan

*I*n her fifteenth year of teaching, on the last day of school—
a fine, spring day when all the world was shiny green and
new life was breaking out wherever one looked, a perfectly splendid day, as last days of school tend to be—Krista
Riley quit her job. She sat at her desk, wrote a letter of resignation, piled the detritus of fifteen years of teaching in a box
that she carried out to her car, and marched into Principal
Dutmire's office before she changed her mind.

Mr. Dutmire, a veteran administrator who tried never to
appear surprised, was stunned. "Quitting? You can't quit.
What will you do? All you've ever done is teach. Is it the
money? If you coached the girls' volleyball team, I could get
you an extra thousand dollars a year. How about it?"

"What I know about volleyball could be put in a thimble,"
Krista said. "Thanks just the same, but I want to go to seminary and be a minister."

"But you're a woman," he said.

"So everyone keeps reminding me," she replied. Then because Mr. Dutmire was a generally kind man and only occasionally officious, Krista smiled and said, "I believe God has called me to ministry not in spite of my being a woman, but because of it."

"I thought you were Catholic," he persisted. "They don't even allow women to be priests."

"Who says I have to stay in the Catholic church? I could be Methodist or Presbyterian, or Quaker for that matter. I might even become one of those snake-handling Pentecostals. They allow women to be ministers."

"You'd change churches?" asked Mr. Dutmire, a man who so resisted change he'd once boasted of eating the same brand of breakfast cereal for thirty-two years.

"People do it every day, most of them for the silliest reasons. I don't see why I can't change to honor my calling."

Principal Dutmire removed his glasses, spritzed them with cleaner he kept in his desk, wiped them clean with his handkerchief, then positioned them carefully behind his ears, the bridge resting just above the notch on his nose, so that he stared over the tops of them at Krista. "Very well. I'll get the paperwork started today."

Then like the fledgling whose first foray from the nest is both frightening and exhilarating, Krista thanked him for understanding, though it was clear he didn't, and walked from the school, her life a delicious swirl of possibility and promise.

• • •

As it turns out, the Methodists didn't work out. Neither did the Presbyterians. They presented her with a numbing list of requirements designed to weed out the feeble and uncommitted. Krista studied their lists, mentally toting up the years before ordination, and concluded she'd be eligible for retirement before she'd preached her first sermon.

The Quakers, however, fewer in number and desperate for new members, received her with open arms.

"We'd be happy to have you attend our seminary," the dean said, walking around his desk and closing the door, lest a prospective minister escape. "We have grants and loans and work-study programs. We can put you right to work. Several small meetings in the area need pastors. You can have your pick."

The Quakers' desperation should have made her suspicious, but after years of hearing NO! to her dream, Krista's jubilation was high, her defenses low, and she enrolled on the spot.

"Classes start the first of September," the dean told her. "Welcome to seminary."

The dean went on, describing the many details of graduate school. Krista took notes, growing dazed by the torrent of information flowing her way.

He paused. "Any questions?"

"Where will I live?" Krista asked. "Is there student housing?"

"Not exactly. But a number of Quakers close to here rent out rooms to our students." He pulled a paper from the top drawer of his desk and ran his finger down a list of names. "Hmm, now, let's see. Frances Drake. No, she's a bit of a crank ... Ginette Wilson. Oh, she passed away. Can't stay with her." He dutifully crossed her name off the list. "Here we go. Ruth Marshal has room. I think you'll get along well with her." He reached over, picked up his phone, and dialed her number. "Yes, Ruth Marshal, this is Dean Mullen."

His destiny apparently determined at birth, the dean of the seminary was aptly named Dean.

"We have a woman student who needs a room. I thought I'd send her over if you're still interested."

Sitting across the room, Krista could hear Ruth Marshal's voice over the phone. "Does she smoke?"

"Do you smoke?" the dean asked Krista.

"No."

"No, she doesn't smoke," the dean reported to Ruth Marshal.

"She doesn't drink, does she?" Ruth Marshal asked.

"How about alcohol?" the dean asked.

"Not so anyone would notice," Krista said, smiling.

"She appears quite sober to me," the dean said over the phone.

"Well, send her over then," Ruth Marshal boomed.

It was only two blocks away, so Krista walked, following the dean's directions. It was a pleasant walk, down a street tunneled in by oaks and maples. Ruth Marshal lived in an old house, a bit worn around the edges, though the hedges were neatly clipped and the lawn freshly mowed. She was seated on the porch swing, awaiting Krista's arrival. She showed her through the front door. The scent reminded Krista of her grandmother's house—a hint of antique dust, English muffins from breakfast, and Murphy's Oil soap.

Ruth guided Krista up a broad walnut staircase that positively gleamed. "You'll have the whole upstairs. A bedroom, a sitting room, and a bath. It's all furnished. We'll share the kitchen and dining room. We clean up after ourselves. And I won't eat your food in the refrigerator if you don't eat mine."

As they toured the three rooms, Ruth Marshal reeled off more rules, all of which sounded tolerable to Krista, though a little persnickety.

"You'll need to close the windows during rainstorms. I do washing on Mondays, so you'll need to have your dirty clothes and bed linens in the basement next to the washer by eight in the morning. Gentleman visitors are confined to the downstairs living room and can stay no later than nine o'clock. And please don't use Comet on the tub and sink. It scratches the finish."

Krista nodded, beginning to wonder what she'd gotten herself into.

"Any questions?" Ruth Marshal asked.

"I think you've covered it all, Mrs. Marshal."

"Call me Ruth. We Quakers don't hold with formalities. Oh, and I almost forgot, we have quiet hours. Radio and TV off by nine o'clock. I like to end my day with peace and quiet."

"I'll probably be studying," Krista said. "Quiet sounds good to me."

"I think we'll get along fine," Ruth Marshal said, shaking Krista's hand solemnly.

"How much is the rent?" Krista asked.

"Two hundred dollars a month, but that includes breakfast and dinner. You're on your own for lunch."

"Oh my, that's very affordable."

"I can charge more if you'd like," Ruth Marshal said, not cracking even the hint of a smile.

"No, two hundred is fine."

The arrangement was solemnized over a glass of iced tea on the front porch.

Krista had a number of questions she wanted to ask Ruth, including whether she was widowed or divorced or hopelessly single like herself. But Krista remembered her lessons from long ago, learned on Mrs. Harvey's front porch, and she steered their conversation toward less private matters—the weather and what Quakers believed and the general state of world affairs. Before Krista realized it, two hours had passed and the ice in her glass had melted to water.

She excused herself to drive home, where she spent the following days sorting and packing and giving away. It was amazing how much she'd accumulated in fifteen years of home ownership. But a yard sale dispersed most of her belongings, and the rest she passed along to her niece. Freed of possessions, she felt light, as if she could take flight and glide among the clouds.

She didn't know much about the Quakers, though Ruth Marshal had spoken a bit about simplicity, of focusing one's life on persons rather than things, and Krista was intrigued by the notion. Of course, now that she was unemployed, simplicity seemed an especially wise choice. Her house sold within three weeks—it was as if God was confirming her plans—and three days before classes began she was comfortably settled in the upstairs of Ruth Marshal's home.

That Sunday morning she went with Ruth to her first Quaker meeting for worship. They began with a hymn—Quakers, she discerned, were not accomplished singers—then settled into silence. A half hour passed with no one saying a word, leaving Krista to wonder what Quaker pastors did and whether they were even necessary. But finally a man, seated on what Ruth Marshal called the "facing bench," stood and spoke on the topic of peace. In his opinion, there wasn't enough of it, and Quakers weren't doing all they could to remedy the situation.

A few people, mostly older men, appeared displeased with his message, and one even stood and said that living in peace wasn't always possible.

"That's George Bales," Ruth Marshal whispered to Krista. "He was in the Second World War. He always speaks whenever the minister preaches on peace."

Listening to their exchange, Krista tried to imagine someone standing during Mass to challenge the Catholic priests she'd known, but couldn't. Quakers were certainly a feisty bunch.

Neither the pastor nor George Bales seemed angry, just sincere, and after a few careful questions they both fell silent. Ten minutes later worship concluded when the pastor rose, walked over to George Bales, and shook his hand.

"I don't get the point of it," Krista said to Ruth Marshal on their walk home from meeting. "He's the pastor, but people obviously don't feel required to do what he says. What's the point of even having a minister?"

"That's an odd question, coming from you."

"What do you mean?" Krista asked.

"You've been told all your life by your pastors that you can't be a priest, yet you felt free to disagree with them and pursue your calling."

"Well, yes, but that's different," Krista said. "They were wrong."

"And who is to judge that? Perhaps they were right. Since we don't know, doesn't it seem wiser to allow each other the privilege of thinking for ourselves?"

"I suppose so," Krista admitted after a moment's thought. "But then why have a pastor?"

"We don't hire pastors to tell us what to do. We invite them to be part of our community and help us think." Ruth Marshal chuckled. "Oh, every now and then we'll get a pastor who tries to boss us around, but we whip them into shape pretty quickly." She leaned closer to Krista, as if confiding a secret. "We Friends don't take kindly to orders and creeds."

Walking along, in the tree-cooled shade, taking care not to trip on a root-heaved piece of sidewalk, Krista had the feeling that whatever she was taught in seminary wouldn't be nearly as helpful as what she would learn from Ruth Marshal.

Eight

A Stirred-up Town

*A*t precisely midnight, just as Sam Gardner had settled into a comfortable sleep after two hours of tossing and turning, the telephone jangled him awake. He grabbed for the handset, which was ordinarily resting on the night table beside his bed, but couldn't find it. It rang a second time, waking his children.

"Where's the phone?" Sam asked his wife, nudging her awake.

"If it isn't on your table, I don't know where it is."

It rang a third time.

"The phone's ringing," their son Addison yelled from his bedroom.

"I'm aware of that," Sam shouted back.

Sam was on his feet, stumbling around their room in the dark, when he stepped squarely on his belt, nearly piercing his foot with the prong of the buckle. He collapsed on the floor in a writhing heap, clutching his foot, muttering a variety of ill-chosen words under his breath.

The phone rang a fourth time.

"Watch your language," Barbara said. "The children are awake."

"I stepped on my belt buckle," Sam said. "I think my foot's bleeding."

"How many times have I told you not to leave your belt on the floor?" she asked.

The phone rang again.

"Can we have this discussion later?" Sam asked. "Why don't you help me find the phone?"

"I remember where it is now. Addison left it on the kitchen table."

Sam raised himself slowly from the floor and hobbled down the stairs to the kitchen, where the phone was indeed lying on the table under the newspaper. It took three more rings for him to find it.

"Hello," he yelled into the phone.

"Hello, this is Dale Hinshaw."

"Hi, Dale," Sam replied, silently seething. Dale Hinshaw! Of course, it would be Dale.

"And I'm calling on behalf of Harmony Friends Meeting to say God loves you and so do we! This is the day the Lord hath made, let us rejoice and be glad in it."

It was Dale, but his voice sounded different, more detached, almost mechanical.

"If you were to die today, do you know where you would spend eternity?" Dale continued.

"Dale, what are you doing? It's midnight. What do you want?"

Dale didn't respond, except to drone on, repeating several Bible verses, inviting Sam to join them for worship at Harmony Friends Meeting the next Sunday at ten-thirty, then disconnecting the call with a firm click.

Sam hung up the phone, though he'd no sooner set it down than it rang again. He snatched it up and stabbed at the talk button. "Hello," he barked into the mouthpiece.

It was Frank, Sam's secretary. "Dale just called me. I think he's gone off the deep end. He sounded funny and wouldn't answer me. He just went on and on about getting saved."

Sam had heard stories about people snapping under the pressures of life and had always suspected Dale was especially at risk.

"Let's talk about it in the morning," he told Frank. "I'd like to get some sleep."

But sleep would not come because of the phone calls that poured into his house. After numerous calls from irate citizens, he took his phone off the hook and fell into bed. By then he was too mad to sleep, and at seven o'clock, his eyes feeling heavy and scratchy as sand, he rolled out of bed, limped to the shower, and prepared for his day, which was already promising to be the worst one of his life.

"Who was that on the phone last night?" Barbara asked at the breakfast table.

"Which time?" Sam grumbled, then yawned.

"I only heard it the one time." It astounded Sam how deeply his wife could sleep.

"We had close to a dozen calls last night," Sam informed her.

"My Lord, who died?"

"No one. Apparently, Dale has had some kind of break-down and started calling people."

"If you had told me someone had gone off the deep end, Dale Hinshaw would have been my first guess," Barbara said, with a sip of her coffee.

"Well, it isn't funny. He got everybody upset, and I couldn't get back to sleep." Sam wondered why people couldn't time their mental breakdowns with more consideration for others.

He finished his breakfast, carried his dishes over to the sink, kissed Barbara good-bye, then walked the three blocks to the meetinghouse. It was a lonely trek. People glared at him from passing cars and shop windows.

Frank met him at the front door. "Dale's in your office," he reported. "And so is Miriam Hodge. And boy, is she mad. I didn't think she ever got mad, but she sure is now. I had to sit Asa Peacock in between her and Dale."

"Asa Peacock's in my office too?"

"Yep, and Owen Stout and Mabel Morrison and Bob Miles."

Sam walked into his office, wading through a sea of human-ity to his desk, where he sat down and invited everyone to do the same.

"Well, what brings you all here?" he asked brightly.

They turned and frowned at Dale.

"Sam, I told 'em you agreed it was a wonderful idea," Dale said.

"Sam, what in the world could you have been thinking?" Miriam Hodge asked, with an uncharacteristic edge to her voice.

"What did I say was a wonderful idea?" Sam asked.

"Our new Scripture greetings ministry," Dale explained. "Remember, I told you all about it. I won the jingle contest, and first prize was a computer disk that had all the phone numbers in the town on it. I just had to record the message and stick it in my computer, and it automatically calls everybody. Slickest thing I've ever seen. Didn't count on this happening, though. You should have warned me, Sam."

"I should have warned you? I had no idea you were doing it."

"See, the problem is that I set it to call everybody at noon, but I couldn't remember if noon is PM or AM. I guess we got it wrong, didn't we, Sam?"

"Dale, stop saying 'we,'" Sam barked.

"It's an outrage," Mabel Morrison sputtered, with a thump of her cane. "Assaulted in our very own homes. I'm on the no-call list, buster. No telephone solicitors can call me. It's against the law. A ten-thousand-dollar fine. And don't think I won't report you to the attorney general. In fact, I already have."

Owen Stout, assuming his lawyerly pose, pulled his reading glasses from the breast pocket of his vest and peered at a sheaf of papers. "Actually, Mabel, as I explained to you earlier, churches are exempt from the state's no-call law. Nevertheless," he said, directing his gaze to Dale, then to Sam, "the church could be sued for harassment."

"That won't be necessary," Sam said. "Dale won't be calling anyone else."

"Well, about that," Dale said. "I've got my computer programmed to call everyone for thirty days. But now that I know noon is PM, I'll get it fixed."

"Dale, I don't want you phoning anyone at midnight or noon," Sam said. "People don't want to be bothered. Take that disk out of your computer and don't do it again."

Sam was having a deeper appreciation for the Luddites every moment and was mightily tempted to take a sledgehammer to Dale's computer.

"Mabel, I'd like to apologize to you on behalf of the church. I can assure you it won't happen again," Miriam Hodge promised.

Mabel, somewhat mollified, rose from her chair. "I guess you can't keep an eye on all the nutcases," she said, glaring at Dale.

Bob Miles, who'd been sitting quietly in the corner taking notes, lifted a camera from a bag at his feet. "While we have everybody here together, let's get a picture for the *Herald*. Everyone give me a big smile. On the count of three. One, two, think of your mother and smile, and three." His flash lit up the room.

"Bob, please don't write about this," Sam pleaded. "The church doesn't need bad press."

"Can I take that as an official 'No comment'?" Bob asked, pulling his notebook from his back pocket.

Sam sighed and glanced at his watch. Eight forty-five and his day had already gone to Hades in a handbasket.

His father had tried to warn him that ministry would be like this. Sam still remembered the day when he'd told his parents he felt called to the pastorate.

His father had buried his face in his hands and groaned in deep, existential pain. "A minister? Why a minister? Why not be a lawyer? You'd make a good lawyer. But a minister? It's the worst job in the world, let me tell you. People calling you all hours of the day, complaining about first one thing and then another. Rotten pay. And forget about job security. You make the wrong person mad and you're out the door like that," he said, with a snap of his fingers.

Sam's mother had smiled sweetly and patted his knee. "It is a rotten job, dear. Are you sure you want to do that with your life?"

"Well, I thought I did," Sam had said.

Now there are days he wishes they'd have clubbed him over the head until he'd come to his senses. Today was one of those days.

Frank shooed everyone from Sam's office, then settled himself into the chair across Sam's desk. "Well, you really blew it this time," he said.

"I didn't do anything," Sam protested. "How come everyone's blaming me?"

"You're the pastor, that's why. Anything bad happens and it's your fault. You ought to know that by now." Frank grinned, clearly enjoying Sam's predicament.

Sam slumped in his chair. "Boy, I work my tail off trying to get this church to grow, trying to attract intelligent, capable people to our meeting, and Dale Hinshaw ruins it all in an hour's time. No one will want to come here now."

"I don't agree, Sam. I think people like Dale will want to come here. They probably liked his phone call."

Sam moaned, barely able to stand the thought of Dale's spiritual cronies filling the meetinghouse.

"The good thing is, people like Dale are tithers," Frank said, trying to look on the bright side. "They pony up the bucks. Maybe now I'll get that raise you've been promising me."

"What's this I hear about you and Miss Rudy?" Sam asked, changing the subject, something he did whenever Frank raised the subject of a pay increase.

Frank bristled. "My personal life is none of your concern."

"So when are you going to make an honest woman out of her?" Sam persisted. "It's not too late for a summer wedding, you know. People your age shouldn't postpone happiness. Never know when you might shuffle off to glory."

"There was a time when ministers were well-mannered," Frank said, stalking out of Sam's office.

"Yeah, and there was a time when church secretaries didn't badger their bosses," Sam yelled back.

They had these spats often, Frank and Sam. They circled one another like two old tomcats, the fight gone out of them but still able to hiss and spit.

Sam busied himself with paperwork for a couple of hours. At eleven-thirty, Frank stuck his head in the office door, somewhat mollified. "How about a little lunch?"

"Coffee Cup?"

"Sounds good to me," Frank said agreeably.

Frank locked the meetinghouse door as they left.

"Why'd you do that?" Sam asked.

"Because it drives Dale nuts," Frank said. "He'll come by and want in and the church will be locked."

"I thought you gave him a key."

"Oh, that. That was the key to my garage, but don't tell him."

Sam chuckled.

"You can't take Dale head-on, Sam. You got to come at him from behind. Wear him down. Make him want to be a Baptist."

That was a sweet thought—Dale Hinshaw joining the Baptist church.

A barrage of protests met them as they entered the restaurant.

"Took me the rest of the night to get back to sleep," Stanley Farlow grumbled. "It's my own church calling me and waking me up. Sixty-seven years I've been a member of that church and my parents before me, and you call and wake me up like that. You oughta be ashamed."

"Sorry about that," Sam said. "Won't happen again."

"Scared the missus half to death," Harvey Muldock muttered. "She thought someone had died. Got her so nervous she couldn't even fix my breakfast. Had to eat out this morning. Oughta send the church the bill, that's what I should do. Makes a fella want to be a Methodist, getting treated like that."

"How about I buy you lunch, Harvey?" Sam offered. Harvey Muldock had given him a pastors' discount on his last car, and Sam wanted to stay in his good graces.

"What about me? You oughta buy my lunch too," Stanley Farlow demanded.

It occurred to Sam that maybe his father was right. He should have been a lawyer. Eight to five. Weekends off. Good pay. As for job security, as long as people bickered, lawyers had it made. Yes, he should have been a lawyer.

He ate his lunch thinking about it. Three years of law school, pass the bar exam, and he'd be well-settled in his new profession by the age of fifty. No more Dale. Sundays off. It was something to think about, anyway.

The remainder of the day passed uneventfully, which set him at ease—a dangerous condition for a minister. By bedtime, he was thoroughly relaxed, which made the impending calamity, when it broke loose in the wee hours of morning, all the more difficult to bear.

Nine
Some Deep Misfortune

That night, as the grandfather clock in Sam and Barbara's living room struck midnight, their phone rang.

"Daggone that Dale anyway," Sam cried out, leaping from his bed to answer the phone before it woke his children.

He didn't bother to say hello, just jabbed at the off button in a vain effort to end the call. Dale's voice droned on, inviting him to worship at Harmony Friends Meeting. Beside himself with fury, Sam beat the telephone into its cradle repeatedly, trying to silence Dale's bland preachments, to no avail.

With a savage tug, he yanked the phone from the wall, stomped downstairs and across the kitchen, threw open the back door, and hurled the phone into the backyard.

"Was that necessary?" Barbara asked, standing at the bottom of the stairs.

Sam looked at her, crazy-eyed and maniacal. "He's done it again. We told him not to call anymore, and he's done it again."

Their kitchen phone rang. "Please don't throw that phone away too. I'd like to have at least one phone in my house."

Sam snatched the phone from the kitchen wall. "Hello," he barked.

"Sam Gardner," Mabel Morrison screeched into his ear, "not sixteen hours ago, you promised that nutcase would stop harassing me. Now you've gone and done—"

Sam hung up, gently this time, and disconnected the phone from the wall jack. He slumped into a kitchen chair, his body aching from spent adrenaline and fury. "I can't take it any longer. I've reached my limit. This is it. I'm quitting."

"Now, now, let's go back to bed. You'll feel better in the morning. A month from now, you and Frank will be laughing about this."

"No, I'm going to Dale's house to cut his phone line."

"Don't be silly. You can't do that. Have another talk with him tomorrow. I'm sure it was just an accident."

He slept fitfully the rest of the night, finally falling into a deep sleep just before his alarm clock rang.

That morning found him showered, shaved, and dressed, standing on Dale Hinshaw's front porch, knocking on his door. Dale answered the door in his pajamas, studying the booklet of instructions from his computer.

"Hey, Sam. Boy, this is the craziest thing," he said, scratching his head. "I know I changed my computer from AM to PM. At least I thought I did. Oh well, just gonna have to keep on trying. Guess that's all we can do. Besides, you know what Paul wrote in his letter to the Hebrews."

"It's a lengthy letter," Sam said. "Perhaps you could be more specific."

"'Run with perseverance the race that is set before us.' We gotta keep persevering."

"Dale, I know you mean well, and don't think I don't appreciate your efforts to help our meeting grow, but you've got to stop. You're making the whole town mad at us. No one's going to come to our church after this."

Dale began to protest, but Sam held up his hand. "Dale, I'm not going to argue with you. You're doing this in the name of the church, and it must stop. If you don't, I'm going to call the elders and have them speak with you."

"Well, that's a fine thing," Dale said. "Somebody in our church finally starts preaching the gospel, and you're gonna have the elders make 'em stop. That's a fine how-do-you-do."

"If you don't like it, you can always attend another church," Sam said.

It had taken him six years to invite Dale to worship else-where, and saying it out loud, instead of muttering it under his breath in private, felt pleasantly liberating.

"And if I left, who would head up our Evangelism Committee?" Dale asked. "Harvey Muldock? Ellis Hodge? I don't think so. They're nice guys, but they don't have the heart for the gospel like I do. No, Sam, I can't leave now. The meeting needs me."

I will have to kill him, Sam thought to himself. It's the only way to be shed of him. Drown him in the bathtub. Load his body in the car trunk and throw him in the river. Maybe Frank can help me. A smile crossed his face.

Dale broke Sam's reverie. "Don't worry, Sam. I'll get it right this time. You just go do your ministry and I'll do mine, and the Lord'll bless us both." And with that, Dale closed the door.

Though Sam didn't think it was possible, the day turned out worse than the one before. Wherever Sam went, he was greeted with open hostility and threats of lawsuits. Two members turned in their membership, and Miriam Hodge, a pacifist to the core, stopped by the office to inform Sam one of his parishioners was in jeopardy. "I'm telling you this now, so you can visit him in the hospital. I'm going to hit Dale Hinshaw squarely in the nose, and I'm not stopping until he's down."

Sam counseled forgiveness and tolerance, but Miriam could tell he was insincere, that he wanted, more than anything else, to clean Dale's clock too.

She had brought a copy of the *Quaker Faith and Practice* with her. "Do you realize there is a glaring omission in our book of order?" she asked Sam. "Nowhere does it say we can kick Dale Hinshaw out of the church."

"I suggested to him that he worship elsewhere," Sam said.

"How'd he take that?"

"He said he could never desert the meeting, that we needed him too badly."

"If I weren't so mad at him, I'd be touched by his loyalty," Miriam said. "Right now, I just want to wrap my hands around that skinny little neck of his, right above his Adam's apple, and squeeze for all I'm worth."

They sat quietly, contemplating the ethereal beauty of such a circumstance.

"Well," Sam said after a bit, "we can't very well do that now, can we?"

"Probably not," Miriam conceded.

"It's times like these that test our Christian charity," Sam pointed out.

"You're absolutely right. I must do better," Miriam said, standing to leave. "Thank you for reminding me of my Christian duty."

Which isn't to say she still didn't want to choke Dale, just that she knew it would be wrong.

After Miriam departed, Frank poked his head in Sam's office door. "Say, uh, Sam, I was thinking of taking tomorrow off. Is that all right with you?"

Sam consulted his pocket calendar, thinking aloud, "Hmm, sermon preparation in the morning ... lunch with the ministers' association ... visitation in the afternoon ... When would you do the bulletin?"

"Already got it done," Frank said. "Stayed over yesterday and wrapped it up. The newsletter's done and mailed out. I have the quarterly reports filled out and put in this morning's mail."

"My, aren't you the picture of efficiency. Sure, you can take the day off. Got big plans?"

Frank hesitated. "I'd rather not say."

"I tell you my secrets."

"No, you don't."

"Yes, I do. Every one of them. I tell you when Barbara's mad at me. You know how much I earn. You know everything about me. I'm an open book. I don't keep anything from you. I can't believe you don't trust me."

"It isn't that I don't trust you. I just don't want you laughing at me," Frank said, with uncharacteristic timidity.

"Frank, I would never laugh at you. You're probably my best friend."

"Well, okay then, I guess it's all right for you to know. Miss Rudy and I are going to Cartersburg to look at a new refrigerator for her."

Sam slapped his desk and began to chuckle. "I knew it. Sounds like it's getting serious. Boy, wait till I tell Barbara."

"Sam Gardner, if you breathe a word of this to anyone, I'll staple your lips shut."

"Oh, don't get your knickers in a twist. I won't tell anyone you and Miss Rudy are shopping for appliances." Sam leaned back in his chair. "Be careful, Frank. This is how desperate women trap a man. They take him shopping for appliances. Innocent on the face of it, but the next thing you know you're picking out china patterns."

"You're not the least bit funny, Sam."

"Hey, Frank. Do me a favor, will you?"

"It depends."

"Find out Miss Rudy's first name, would you? I've known her all my life, and I still don't know her first name."

"I know it," Frank said. "She told me."

"What is it?"

"I promised not to tell and, unlike some people I could mention, I know how to keep a secret."

"If you marry her and I do the wedding, I'll have to know her first name to fill out the wedding license," Sam pointed out.

"Maybe we'll just live together and scandalize everyone," Frank said. "Just think how much trouble that would cause you. Fern Hampton would be all over you, wanting you to fire me. It would make this mess with Dale Hinshaw look like a picnic."

Sam paled. "You wouldn't do that to me, would you, Frank?"

"In a minute. Yep, they'd fire me and hire Dale Hinshaw to be your new secretary, seeing how he has his own computer. You'd make a good team, you and Dale."

Sam felt the faint stirring of nausea.

For a church secretary, Frank had a cruel streak that showed itself at the worst times.

"Take the day off, then," Sam grumbled. "It'll be nice to have the place to myself for a day."

"With or without pay?"

"Without!"

"You give it to me with pay and if I marry Miss Rudy, I'll tell you her first name."

"Deal," Sam said.

"Where we gonna eat lunch?"

"Barbara packed something for me. There's no way I'm going out in public. Not after Dale woke up the whole town last night."

Sam worked until late afternoon, then walked home down the alleyways, keeping to the shadows so no one would see him. He was almost home when Shirley Finchum, burning trash in her backyard barrel, spied him. "Sam Gardner, you're just the man I wanted to see." She wagged her cane at him. "Two nights now I've been woken up. What are you going to do about that?"

"My apologies, Mrs. Finchum. It won't happen again. I'd love to stay and visit, but I've got to get home." He hurried across his backyard, around the garage, up the back steps, and through the screen door into the kitchen.

"This day can't end too soon," he told Barbara, collapsing into a kitchen chair.

She presented him with a long list of phone messages. "Thirteen phone calls. Not one of them from a happy person. I told them you'd call them back when you got home tonight."

Sam groaned. "Oh, for Pete's sake, why did you do that? I don't want to call these people. They're just gonna yell at me."

He ate supper to boost his strength, then returned the phone calls, holding the phone away from his ear to protect his hearing. For a Christian town, people were startling in their ferocity, threatening Sam and the meeting with all manner of misfortune if he dared disturb their sleep again.

"It wasn't me," Sam tried to explain. "Dale Hinshaw's doing this on his own. We told him not to." But that made little difference, and after five calls Sam called it a night.

Before he went to sleep, he had the foresight to take his one remaining phone off the hook. He was asleep by nine-thirty, his body occasionally twitching, haunted by nightmares of Dale Hinshaw taking up residence as the new secretary of Harmony Friends. At the stroke of midnight, Sam sat bolt upright in bed, sensing some deep misfortune had been unleashed in his life. The house was perfectly quiet, except for the tick of the clock downstairs. He lay back down, staring at the ceiling, perceiving his world had shifted, though not knowing how and in no way eager to find out.

Ten

The Rock That Cracked

I f Gloria Gardner had heard her husband say it once, she'd heard him say it a thousand times. "I tell you, I got the worse luck of anyone I know. It's like I got a cloud hangin' over my head. If it isn't one thing, it's another. Some days I wonder why I even bother to get out of bed."

He always said this within her earshot, and she'd grown immune to his lamentations and no longer took them personally.

The testimony of the years seemed to bear him out: he was routinely audited by the IRS; while attending the seventh game of the 1960 World Series, he was beaned by a foul ball and remained unconscious the rest of the game; a year later he was struck by lightning and had been afflicted by static electricity ever since. His hair was a sight; people wouldn't shake his hand for fear of being shocked. And he was strip-searched every time he flew, owing to his tendency to set off metal detectors just by walking near them.

But all those were mere inconveniences compared to what befell her husband that night, for at the stroke of midnight, when every phone in town was off the hook, lest the citizenry be plagued by Dale's telephone evangelism, Charlie Gardner had a heart attack. His arms flailed about, striking his wife, who came up out of bed, thinking the phone had rung.

"That darn Dale. He's pestering us again," she muttered.

Charlie gurgled, then went rigid. His eyes rolled back in his head, making them look like two white marbles, the big kind, the shooters.

"Oh, Lord," Gloria cried. "Oh, my."

"Call Sam," Charlie gasped.

She hurried from their bedroom to the phone in the kitchen, but couldn't for the life of her remember Sam's number. She ran back into their bedroom. "I can't think straight. What's his number?"

"Fleetwood 96701," Charlie whispered.

Everyone in town had the same prefix. Folks over seventy remembered it as Fleetwood, while the youngsters rattled off the numbers.

She ran back in the kitchen and punched in Sam's number. A groggy voice answered the phone. "Yeah."

"Sam, get over here quick, your father's dying."

"You got the wrong number, lady. There's no Sam here."

She let out an anguished wail.

Charlie stumbled from the bedroom into the hallway, clutching his chest, the heart attack stepping up his static electricity so that he looked like Albert Einstein, his hair jutting out and fairly crackling. He lurched down the hallway toward her. "Give me the phone," he whispered.

He studied the keypad, dialed Sam's number, and was rewarded with a frantic beeping. "Busy? Who in the world could he be talking to this time of night?"

Another spasm struck him, and he fell to one knee. "Call Johnny Mackey," he wheezed, his voice the texture of broken glass.

Ironically, not five years before, Charlie Gardner had led the charge against the town installing 911 service. "For crying out loud, if we got problems, we can dial four extra numbers. What's the big deal? How long can that take?" A few naysayers can keep an entire populace in the Dark Ages and his voice, along with that of Dale Hinshaw, who'd spoken at length against the one-world government, had been enough to scotch the enterprise.

"What's Johnny Mackey's number?" Gloria asked. "Where's the phone book?"

But Charlie's sun was setting in the west, and he didn't respond.

In the end, she ran across the street to Harvey Muldock's, who phoned Johnny Mackey, the town mortician and owner of the sole ambulance in a twenty-mile radius. Unfortunately, having been wakened from his slumber the past two nights by Dale's phone ministry, Johnny, like the rest of the town, had taken his phone off the hook.

That left Harvey Muldock to load Charlie in the backseat of his car and drive the twenty-five miles with Gloria to

Cartersburg. Every mile or so, he would reach into the back-seat and thump Charlie sharply on the chest and shout encouragement. "Hang in there, buddy. We're almost there."

When they arrived at the hospital, Charlie was stiff as a fish, his skin a moonlike, ghastly white.

Sam, back at his house, was up and pacing, sensing danger, his mind dismissing one possibility even as another rushed to fill the void. He studied his wife and sons to see if they were breathing. He walked through the house checking the doors, then went outside and walked the perimeter of his home. Everything seemed fine. No fire, no burst water pipes, no serial killer crouching in the bushes waiting to maim his family.

He heard the slight scuff of shoes against pavement and saw a motion in the corner of his vision. My Lord, he was about to be mugged. Probably beaten within an inch of his life. Maybe even killed. He'd read numerous newspaper stories of such things, though they usually happened in places far from Harmony, which meant they were overdue here.

A lifetime of Quaker pacifism had rendered him defenseless in such matters, and he fell to the ground where he curled in a ball, his hands covering his head.

"Sam!"

The mugger knew his name. A killer in their midst all these years.

"Sam, it's me, Eunice Muldock. What are you doing on the ground?"

"Checking for aphids," Sam said. "They've infested our roses. What are you doing out this time of night?"

"It's your father. Something's wrong with him. They tried calling you, but couldn't get through. Harvey's taking him to the hospital."

"Dad? What's wrong with him?"

"We don't know. Your mom thought maybe he'd had a heart attack. He looks pretty bad. Now when Harvey had his heart attack, he didn't even know it. He thought it was gas. Then later on they ran a test on him, and it showed he'd had a heart attack. He thinks he had it shoveling snow, but he's not sure. So now he doesn't shovel snow. We have the Grant boy shovel our walks. 'Course a young fella like you can shovel your own snow, but when you get to be as old as us, you got to hire it done."

This was typical of emergencies in Harmony. A house could erupt in flames, spitting fireballs and igniting every residence within a hundred yards, and the neighbors would stop the fire-fighters to chat about past infernos. "Yeah, now this here, it's a pretty good fire, but I remember in 1964, no, it was '63, when Myron Farlow's barn went up. You could see the flames all the way into town. Boy, now that was some fire. Bubbled the paint on the water tower half a mile away, I swear to God. Fires, they burnt a lot hotter back in those days. These fires today, I don't know, they just don't seem all that hot."

While Eunice chattered on, Sam turned and rushed into his house, up the stairs into their bedroom, where he proceeded to pull on his clothes. He roused Barbara from her sleep. "Dad's been taken to the hospital. I'm going down there. You stay here with the boys, and I'll call you when

I find something out. Put the phone back on the hook. See you later." He bent down and kissed her good-bye, hoping his words had registered with her.

On the drive to Cartersburg, his mind was in turmoil contemplating his father's death. Barbara had been urging him to spend more time with his father, which he'd neglected to do, even after his father had invited him to go on a fishing trip. "Dear Lord, please let him live. I'll spend all my time with him. Just let him live." He prayed aloud the entire way, driving as fast as he dared on the twisty, narrow country roads.

Harvey and his mother were in the emergency room when he arrived. His mother was a knot of worry, twisting her hands and peering every few seconds at the doors, willing a doctor to emerge with good news. Sam rushed to her side and hugged her. "What's wrong? How's Dad?"

"Oh, Sam, it was awful. He's all pale and everything."

"That's the funny thing about it," Harvey piped up. "I turned red when I had my heart attack. Came in from shoveling snow just as red as a tomato. I remember because Eunice took one look at me and said, 'Harvey Muldock, you're red as a tomato.' Now I didn't know at the time I'd had a heart attack, but they say I did. So I don't shovel snow anymore. You know who shovels our snow?"

"The Grant boy."

"That's right. How'd you know that?"

"Just a lucky guess," Sam said.

"He does a pretty good job, I suppose. 'Course he ought to for what I pay him. Ten dollars."

Sam turned to his mother. "Have you talked with the doctors yet? What are they saying?"

"Not yet. We've only been here a little while. They said it might be an hour before they knew something."

"We made pretty good time," Harvey said proudly. "Thirty-four minutes, door to door. That's going the short way, past the Hodges'. What way did you come?"

"Same way."

Harvey leaned back in his chair. "Now I remember when my Uncle Harvey had his heart attack. I was named for him, you know. Anyway, it was the second day of July, nineteen and sixty-nine. We went that way and the bridge was out just past the Hodges' place. You know that bridge, there over White Lick Creek. Big storm that day had knocked the bridge out. Ten inches of rain, most rain we ever had. That's how I remembered the date. Anyway, we had to turn around and bring him back through town and take the long way past Jessups' farm and through Tilden. Fifty-six minutes it took us that time. He nearly died. He looked the same as your Dad. That's how I knew your Dad was in bad shape, on account of it happening to my uncle."

He paused to breathe and was commencing to launch into a detailed review of other heart attack victims he'd known when Sam cut him short.

"Sure appreciate you bringing Mom and Dad down here, Harvey. Eunice seemed awful worried, so maybe you ought to go back and be with her. I'll call you just as soon as we find something out."

"Oh, I can wait," Harvey assured Sam. "Besides, I'm curious to see how things turn out."

Heart attacks, Sam had learned over the years, were a spectator sport in certain Harmony circles. Like veterans swapping stories of their army days, Harvey and the old men of the Coffee Cup regaled one another with tales of aortic embolisms and arteriosclerosis. Sam wasn't anxious for his father to be the heart du jour at the Coffee Cup. He placed his hand under Harvey's elbow and helped him to his feet. "We'll be talking with you then, Harvey. Thanks again for all your help."

"Anytime, Sam. You call me anytime you need me."

"Thank you, Harvey," Gloria Gardner added. "You're a good neighbor."

"Well, we do what we can," Harvey said modestly, pulling his pants higher with a mighty tug. Harvey Muldock had the highest waistline of anyone in town; his belt landed scant inches below his armpits. "You keep in touch now."

"Will do," Sam assured him.

Sam and his mother sat quietly in the waiting room. A man entered after a while, pressing a bloody bandage to his arm. A nurse whisked him away.

"Wonder what happened to him?" Sam said.

"Maybe he's a burglar and he cut his arm breaking out a window," his mother speculated.

"Could be he got hurt rescuing a small child," Sam said, trying to be positive.

"I bet he got drunk and got cut in a bar fight."

"Mother, let's try being a little more charitable, shall we."

It felt odd scolding his mother. Then again, he was her pastor, and it was his job to appeal to her nobler qualities.

"You're absolutely right," she said, patting his hand. "You're a good minister, son."

"Thank you, Mom."

The double doors opened with a whoosh of air; a doctor walked into the waiting room and came toward them. "Mrs. Gardner?"

"Yes, that's me." Sam's mother rose to greet him. "This is my son, Sam. He's a minister."

The doctor smiled politely and shook Sam's hand. "Well, the Lord must have heard your prayers. It looks like your father's going to make it."

"Thank God," they chorused.

"He's not out of the woods, but he is stable. He's going to need a bypass operation. We don't do that here, of course. He'll need to go to the city. My nurse is going to work with you to set up a date for that. Sooner the better, though."

Sam reached his arm around his mother and pulled her to him.

"Thank you, Lord," he whispered. But even as he prayed, he knew the landscape of his world had altered, that the rock who'd been his father had cracked and no mortar on God's earth, however strong, could repair it.

Eleven

Sam Takes Leave

"What do you mean, you need three months off?" Dale Hinshaw screeched at the Harmony Friends monthly business meeting.

"I want to care for my father," Sam said, with a calmness he didn't feel. "He and my mother need my help."

"I suppose he'll want it off with pay," Stanley Farlow muttered to no one in particular, though making sure everyone heard it.

"In the olden days," Sam said, with an appeal to tradition, "pastors took several months off each summer for rest and renewal. I've been here six years, now my father needs me, and I'd like to help him."

"It's fine with me," Asa Peacock said. "I let a field lie fallow every now and then. Don't see why Sam can't take some time off. Especially to help his father."

Dale frowned, then began thumbing through his Bible. "I'd ask you to consider the ninth chapter of Luke's Gospel, verses fifty-nine and sixty. 'And he said unto another, "Follow me." But the man said, "Lord, suffer me first to go and bury my father." Jesus said unto him, "Let the dead bury their dead: but go thou and preach the kingdom of God."' Well, there you have it, Sam. Do you want to follow Jesus or your father? Seems pretty clear to me."

Everything was clear to Dale Hinshaw, which was another reason Sam needed time off.

"Does anyone else have a leading on this?" Miriam Hodge, the clerk, asked.

"I'll tell you my leading," Dale chimed in.

"We're well aware of your thoughts on the matter, Dale. Let's give someone else the opportunity to speak."

"I'm against it," he continued. "Faith is what Sam needs. Not time off."

He turned to Sam. "Nothing personal. Just trying to keep you on the narrow way that leads to heaven."

Miriam's hands twitched, forming a choking motion.

"I say we give Sam three months off," Jessie Peacock said. "With pay. He's more than earned it."

"Friend Jessie speaks my mind," Judy Iverson said. Judy could always be depended upon to be charitable.

They sat in silence for several moments. Miriam searched each face, gauging the mood, then proceeded carefully. "Are Friends clear that we should offer Sam Gardner three months off to care for his father? With pay."

"If you ask me, it's a big mistake," Dale said.

"We're not asking you," Jessie Peacock said. "So zip it." Jessie had been awakened the past three nights by Dale's telephone ministry, and the lack of sleep had apparently made her edgy.

"When would he start?" Opal Majors asked.

"His father needs help now, so I imagine immediately," Miriam answered.

"Who'll be our minister while he's gone?" Asa Peacock asked.

"For our first two hundred years, Quakers didn't have pastors. Surely, we can minister to one another for three months," Miriam suggested.

"Sounds like a lot of work to me," Stanley Farlow grumbled.

"Or," Miriam continued, "we could phone the superintendent and see if the seminary has a student minister who might join us for that short time."

"A new minister," Asa Peacock said. "That sounds interesting. Let's do that."

The room buzzed with anticipation of a fresh face, all the other fresh faces having fled.

"Are Friends agreed we should release Sam for three months with pay and that I should contact the superintendent and ask for an interim pastor while Sam is gone?" Miriam asked.

"Approved," they chorused, and with that Sam Gardner was a free man.

Miriam phoned the superintendent the next morning and explained their need.

"Got just the man for you," he told her. "In fact, I believe you've met him. I'm thinking of my nephew."

Miriam had indeed met his nephew and had been singularly underwhelmed.

"Actually, we had something else in mind. We'd like you to contact the seminary and arrange for a student pastor to be with us."

"You sure about that? You know these students nowadays. They're awful liberal."

"Nevertheless, that's what our monthly meeting approved."

"So be it. I'll call Dean, and we'll send you over a nice young man."

"Why does it have to be a man?" Miriam asked. "We don't care about gender. We want competence."

"Does Dale know this?"

"It's time Dale Hinshaw learned he's not the only person in our congregation."

Dale, she was sure, would fly into fits if they hired a woman pastor, which made Miriam all the more determined. "In fact, I think we'd prefer a woman. It's time we broadened our horizons. Yes, you tell Dean Mullen we'd like a woman pastor."

"Dale won't like this," the superintendent warned.

"What Dale Hinshaw likes or doesn't like is of little concern to me these days," Miriam said. "He hasn't exactly endeared himself to the rest of us lately."

Later, Miriam would wonder if wanting to provoke Dale had been worth it. But for now, she was quietly pleased at the prospect of irritating him.

Had she not lost her objectivity, she would even have concluded that her behavior was no better than Dale's. But revenge is a sweet dish when eaten warm, and Miriam Hodge was hungry.

• • •

On the second day of class, Krista Riley was summoned to Dean Mullen's office. It felt a bit like being called before the principal, like being ten years old and ordered to report for a stern lecture. But Dean Mullen greeted her with a smile and ushered her into his office. "Sit, please sit. Can I get you something to drink? Perhaps you'd like a donut."

"No, thank you."

"Coffee?"

"That would be nice, thank you. A little sugar, please."

Dean Mullen poured two cups of coffee and carefully placed Krista's on the table beside her chair.

He sat across from her, eased back in his chair, and smiled pleasantly, his eyes crinkling. "Well, Krista, how are your studies?"

"So far I enjoy them, though I had no idea there'd be this much reading."

The dean chuckled. "Yes, well, it pays to sharpen your scythe before the harvest. And speaking of harvest, we have an opportunity for you."

"An opportunity?"

"Yes, I got a phone call today from the superintendent of the yearly meeting. Seems one of our meetings is in need of a pastor. Place called Harmony, a couple hours from here. Their regular pastor, Sam Gardner, is taking the next three months off. His dad had a heart attack, and they need his help."

"That seems like a lot of driving each day."

"You wouldn't go there every day. Many of our students pastor churches at a distance. They drive to their churches on Thursday after class and come back here on Sunday afternoon."

"If I took the job, where would I stay?"

"I've been told they have a furnished apartment for you."

"When would I do my studying?" Krista asked.

"As you had time, same as everyone else."

"What can you tell me about the meeting?"

The dean hesitated. "Well, it's in a nice little town. Very peaceful, a quiet town."

"Yes, but what about the congregation? What are they like?"

"Tremendous cooks," Dean Mullen said. "They have a Chicken Noodle Dinner every year that'll knock your socks off."

"So it's a peaceful town with good cooks."

"You've got it!" exclaimed the dean. "That sums it up nicely."

Krista sighed. "What kind of church is it? Progressive? Traditional? Middle-of-the-road?"

"It's rather hard to say. It defies an easy description."

"But it's just for three months?"

"Yes, ma'am. Three months, that's all. Meanwhile, you'll gain some experience and earn a little spending money. Interested?"

Krista sipped her coffee and sat quietly, thinking, then asked, "Have they ever had a woman pastor?"

"I don't think so. But when I told them about you, their clerk seemed intrigued. They've got a lot of strong women in that meeting, so I don't think it'll be a problem. In fact, I think you'll fit right in."

"When would they like me to start?"

"Now."

"I'll do it," Krista said, abandoning her usual discretion with a leap into the unknown.

"Fine, then," Dean Mullen said. "I'll give them a call and tell them the good news. I'm sure they'll be delighted."

Krista left Dean Mullen's office excited, though with a trace of concern. The dean had seemed rather vague about Harmony Friends. Oh well, she thought, it's only three months. What can go wrong in three months?

She spent the rest of her day in classes, then hurried home to Ruth Marshal's and began writing her first sermon. Although she'd written dozens of sermons, this would be the first one people would hear. She resisted the urge to dump a full load on them and decided instead to use their initial meeting to introduce herself, reliable information being preferable to speculative gossip.

That evening, after supper, while she and Ruth Marshal were drinking iced tea on the front porch, she spilled the beans. "I've been given my first church. It's just for three months, filling in for a pastor who's caring for his parents."

"Well, what fine news that is!" Ruth Marshal exclaimed. "It sounds like a wonderful opportunity. What meeting is it?"

"It's a few hours from here. Harmony Friends Meeting."

"Oh, my. Well, as you said, it's only for three months."

"What do you mean by that?" Krista asked.

"Nothing at all, dear. You'll love it there. It's a pleasant little town, very peaceful. Wonderful cooks, from what I understand. Care for more tea?"

"No, thank you."

Krista had more questions but was afraid to ask them for fear she might not like the answers.

"There's a man there," Ruth Marshal said, tentatively. "He's rather odd. I don't know him well, but one hears things." She paused, as if trying to determine whether she should continue, then plunged ahead. "I really shouldn't tell you this. It feels like gossiping, but I think you should know."

"What should I know?"

"Again, I don't know this man well. I've only spoken with him once, but I've observed him at yearly meeting for many years now. His name is Dale Hinshaw."

"What about him?"

"To put it simply, he's a kook."

"Hmm," Krista said, letting this revelation sink in. "Surely they know that about him and don't let him run things."

Ruth Marshal chose her words carefully. "Krista, you will learn, if you haven't already, that churches are vulnerable to domineering people. Even if they aren't officially given power, these people find a way to get it."

"Schools are much the same way," Krista said. "I suppose that's true of any human institution."

"But it's especially tragic in the church. These people earnestly believe they speak for God, and it causes much harm."

"I suppose I can handle anything for three months," Krista said. "Even this Dale Hinshaw."

"Poor habits formed early in one's ministry have a way of establishing themselves. It's important you handle this well."

"I'll keep that in mind," Krista promised.

"Be loving, be honest, and be yourself," Ruth Marshal said, reaching across to squeeze her hand, "and you'll do just fine."

Despite Ruth Marshal's misgivings, Krista was elated at the prospect of pastoring her own church and phoned her parents to tell them the good news. Her father had his doubts, attributing her foray into ministry to a premature midlife crisis. Her mother, however, was genuinely thrilled. "Oh, honey. I'm so happy for you. You've wanted this so long. When do you start?"

"This Sunday."

"What will you preach about?" her mother asked.

"I thought I'd use the opportunity to introduce myself."

"Wonderful thinking. I'm sure they'll fall in love with you. Oh, Krista, I'm so proud of you."

It is breathtaking to be called by a church to ministry, though the approval of one's mother runs a close second, and when Krista hung up the phone, she was filled with a profound joy.

Had she known the events leading up to her call, she might have been less thrilled, but ignorance being bliss, she couldn't wait until Sunday.

Twelve

Krista Comes to Town

Krista Riley arrived in Harmony on Friday a little before noon and, faced with the choice of lunch at the Coffee Cup or the Legal Grounds Coffee Shop, she chose the former and consequently became the topic of the day.

It had been 1962 since a woman had dared cross the Coffee Cup's sacred threshold to eat lunch. It was done in protest by the late Juanita Harmon, who in a bold strike for women's rights, marched in, took a seat at the lunch counter, and wouldn't leave until she'd been served. One taste of the food convinced her there were better ways to fight for equality.

There are, of course, exceptions to the no-woman edict. Penny Torricelli is permitted access, since she and her husband, Vinny, do the cooking. Heather Darnell is the waitress and resident eye candy, so the men welcome her presence. Bea Majors plays the organ on Italian Night, when it is generally understood that women are welcome—Wednesday nights, five to seven.

But not in recent memory had a woman entered the Coffee Cup at lunchtime for the express purpose of dining. All over the restaurant, forks were laid down and voices fell silent.

"Would you look at that?" Stanley Farlow said. "It's a woman."

There had to be a reasonable explanation. Perhaps she was a stranger traveling through, lost, in need of directions.

"Can I help you?" Vinny asked.

"Yes, I'd like iced tea, a grilled chicken breast sandwich"— all over the Coffee Cup men blushed at hearing a woman say the word "breast"—"and a fruit dish," Krista said, smiling pleasantly.

"Most of the women, they like eating at the Legal Grounds," Vinny said quietly.

"Oh, not me. I like diners. And this is quite a lovely one." Then, to the utter astonishment of everyone present, she crossed the room and sat down in Asa Peacock's booth.

"Uh, that seat's taken," Vinny explained.

"I don't see anyone sitting here."

"Asa, he doesn't get here till after noon. He likes listening to the farm report first. But that's his booth. He always sits there."

"It's a large booth," Krista pointed out. "He probably doesn't take up the whole table, does he?"

Dale Hinshaw was ready to faint dead away. This, he knew, was the beginning of the end, yet another sign of the impending apocalypse. It was all there in the Bible—the rise of the nation Israel, the coming of the Antichrist, and one-world government culminating in a woman eating lunch at the Coffee Cup.

He approached Krista cautiously, fearing she might sprout claws and slice him to shreds. "Dale Hinshaw's my name. Don't believe I've seen you around here before."

"There's a reason for that," Krista said.

"There is?"

"Yes, I've never been here." She offered her hand to Dale, who after some hesitation, shook it briefly. "My name is Krista Riley. I'm your new pastor."

Witnesses, recounting the story later, would say they never saw Dale even open the door, so quick was his exit. "It was a blur, everything happened so fast," Stanley Farlow told Bob Miles from the *Herald*. "At first, he just backed up a few steps, then he turned white and lit out like a scared rabbit."

Within two minutes, he'd reached Sam's home, where Barbara greeted him at the door.

"We got ourselves a problem. Is Sam here?"

"No, he isn't, Dale. He's over at his parents' house. If this is church business, he's not available. He's on sabbatical. You'll have to see the new pastor."

"That's our problem!" Dale shrieked. "They sent us a woman! We got ourselves a woman minister. They put a woman in charge of us."

"It's about time," Barbara said, closing the door.

There was nothing like sacrilege to put a spring in Dale's step, and he was home within five minutes. Seated at his desk, he began compiling a list of grievances he could nail to the meetinghouse door.

"A woman minister!" he screeched repeatedly. "They sent us a woman minister. Can you believe that?"

"Women do all sorts of things now," Dolores Hinshaw said, in a vain effort to settle him down. "They even have women firemen."

Dale fixed her with a glare. "There is nothing in the Bible that says a woman can't be a fireman. But the Scriptures are clear on women pastors. First Timothy, chapter 2, verse 12." He eyed her suspiciously. "You don't seem very upset about this."

"It's only for three months. Besides, I think it'll be interesting to hear a woman preach." Every now and then, to Dale's distress, Dolores Hinshaw rummaged around, found her backbone, and spoke her mind.

"Well, you won't be hearing a woman preach, because she's leaving," he declared emphatically.

Within a half hour, word of Krista Riley's arrival had circulated through town. Bob Miles arrived from the *Herald* just in time to photograph her eating the last of her chicken sandwich, which, to Vinny and Penny's delight, she pronounced the finest chicken sandwich she'd eaten in some time.

"How did you prepare that?" she asked Vinny. "It had such a delicate flavor."

Unaccustomed to compliments, Vinny blushed, then stammered, "I don't know what they put on it. I get it frozen from the warehouse."

"The secret must be in the grilling then," Krista said. "It was simply delicious."

New woman pastor declares Coffee Cup sandwich best she's ever eaten, Bob Miles scribbled in his notebook. She must not get out much, he thought to himself.

"So where you from?" Bob asked, rooting for more information.

"Right here in Indiana, from Danville, up in Hendricks County," Krista said.

"How long have you been a pastor?"

She glanced at her watch. "Three days, two hours, and eleven minutes."

"You're the first woman minister we've had in our town," Bob said, studying her with a mixture of fascination and curiosity, like one would scrutinize a two-headed turtle. "What does your husband think of you being a minister?"

"If I ever have one, I'll ask him and see," Krista said.

"Hmm, not married. Very interesting. Well, maybe you'll meet someone while you're here." He turned to Vinny and Penny. "Did you hear that? She's not married."

"I don't know how you've lived this long without the pleasure of washing a man's underwear," Penny said.

Vinny and Bob frowned.

"Well, don't you worry about it," Bob said. "Once the bachelors in our town find out you're available, you'll have to swat them away like flies."

New woman minister seeks helpmate, he wrote in his notebook.

"Actually, I'm not interested in dating just now," Krista said. "I'm quite busy with school, plus I have a job."

"You should never be too busy for romance," Vinny said.

Penny snorted. "What do you know about romance? Just last week I asked you to whisper something nice in my ear and you talked about baseball."

"What's wrong with baseball? Baseball is nice," Vinny grumbled.

Argument erupts as new pastor arrives in town, Bob scribbled in his notebook.

"It's been a pleasure meeting all of you, but I must go now," Krista said, rising from her seat. "I have an appointment at the meetinghouse."

"Best of luck to you," Bob Miles said. "I think you're gonna like it here. They've got some wonderful cooks at that church."

"So I've heard."

"It's been a pleasure visiting with you," Krista said, shaking Bob's hand. "And Vinny and Penny, thank you for a lovely lunch." She gazed around the Coffee Cup, taking in the swordfish mounted on the back wall over the salad bar, its blue skin casting an aqua glow on the wilted lettuce. "Simply lovely. That's all I can say."

She paid her bill, left a generous tip, and with a wave of her hand slipped out the door.

"That right there is enough to make anyone become a Christian," Vinny Torricelli said. "A true lady."

"I can't remember the last time Sam Gardner said anything nice about our food," Penny said.

"He's not much of a tipper either," Vinny added.

Finding the meetinghouse was not at all difficult. The door was unlocked, so Krista entered and called out, "Anyone home?"

"Down here," a voice yelled back.

She walked down the stairs to the basement. It smelled musty; a faint odor of noodles permeated the air. "Hello."

"In here, for crying out loud."

That's when she noticed a door, set back in a shadowed corner. She opened it slowly. A lone lightbulb hung over what appeared to be a janitor's sink. A gnarled, elderly gentleman wearing paint-spattered pants was filling a coffeepot.

"Are you the janitor?" Krista asked.

"Nope, the secretary. Name's Frank."

He turned to shake her hand. He had a profusion of hair growing from his ears, giving him an owl-like appearance.

She didn't miss a beat. "Yes, of course. I'm Krista Riley, the new pastor."

"Been expecting you."

"Well, yes, uh, is Pastor Gardner here?"

"Nope. Probably over at his parents' house. His father had a heart attack, you know."

"Yes, I heard."

Frank finished filling the coffeepot and turned off the spigot. "Care for some coffee?"

"No thank you."

She followed him up the stairs into his office. "We were supposed to meet at one o'clock."

"He'll be here then. Sam says he'll be somewhere at one o'clock, he'll be there. You can wait for him in his office, if you want."

"I thought I might look around the meetinghouse."

"Suit yourself," Frank said. "But stay out of the noodle freezers. It upsets the ladies something terrible."

Interesting man, she thought to herself. He was certainly different from any church secretary she'd ever met.

She walked in the meeting room. It was quite lovely—a high-ceilinged room with pale blue walls that contrasted handsomely with the cherrywood pews. The carpet and hymnals appeared new. She walked forward down the aisle, her senses sharp, and took a seat behind the pulpit. In the quiet, she could hear the rhythmic tick of the clock across the room. Three large windows lined each side of the meeting room. The north windows looked out upon the town's main street. An occasional car flashed past. The windows across the meeting room offered a view of a rolling meadow, speckled with bales of hay waiting to be gathered. Off in the distance a stream draped around the field like a necklace.

She walked over to the window and gazed out at the field, watching a half dozen buzzards circle on the thermal winds, waiting for something to die.

"Pretty, isn't it?" a voice behind her said.

Startled, she turned around to find a thin-haired, tallish man looking at her, his hand outstretched.

"I'm Sam."

"Oh, yes. Hello, Sam. I'm Krista Riley," she said, shaking his hand. "It's a pleasure to meet you. I was sorry to hear of your father. How is he?"

"Recovering, but slowly. We'll know he's better when he starts grouching at my mom."

Krista laughed. "It sounds like our fathers are cut from the same cloth."

"Have you met Frank?"

"Yes. He's certainly, uh—"

"Interesting," Sam suggested.

"Yes, that's just what I was thinking."

"I think you'll like him. He's a good guy, but he wouldn't want anyone to know that."

"At first, I thought he was the janitor."

Sam chuckled. "That's what he gets. I've told him to dress nicer, but he never listens."

Sam showed her around the meetinghouse, pointing out the various curiosities—the framed pictures of the 1926 centennial picnic, the Frieda Hampton Memorial Clock, the noodle table, and the chart in the entryway that showed they'd raised $112.59 for their building fund.

"Oh, are you building a new meetinghouse?" Krista asked.

"Not planning on it. We thought we'd start a fund just in case."

"Well, it appears you're off to a grand start," Krista said.

"Never hurts to plan ahead," Sam said. "Come on, I'll show you the office."

Frank was seated at his desk. "So you're our new minister, eh? Well, you're a darn sight prettier than our old one, let me tell you."

Krista blushed, Sam and Frank laughed, and in the warmth of their fellowship Krista Riley felt she'd come home.

Thirteen

Mr. Sunshine

Charlie Gardner reclined in his La-Z-Boy watching *Jeopardy* and matching wits against an Iowa schoolteacher.

"Iwo Jima, for crying out loud. She's a teacher, she oughta know that. Boy, I wish they'd put me on that show. I'd be set for life. Hey, Sam, bring me a little more iced tea."

Three weeks had passed since Charlie's heart bypass operation, and Sam Gardner was quickly losing all sympathy for his stricken father. In addition to yelling at his television, he'd been barking orders right and left. Sam and his mother were exhausted. Earlier that day, Charlie had caught them in the bedroom closet plotting a coup, scheming to exile him to the rehab center in Cartersburg. He'd fought back, employing the divide-and-conquer strategy, booting Sam outside to pull weeds and ordering Gloria to the Kroger to buy more Cheetos and Dr. Pepper.

Sam phoned the doctor to discuss his father's temperament, explaining that he'd turned into a tyrant.

"Mood swings aren't uncommon," the doctor said. "Some patients become depressed, others become more mellow, but some become demanding and very stubborn."

"How long will that last?"

"Hard to say. He could be his old self tomorrow. Then again, he could stay this way for years. Maybe he should go for counseling."

"Fat chance of that happening," Sam said.

Sam had suggested that very thing the week before, and Charlie had hit the roof.

"So now you think I'm crazy. Is that what you're saying? I know what you want. You want to get me committed to a nuthouse and get all my money. That's what you want."

Then he'd sent Sam outside to clean the gutters. Sam wasn't surprised. He knew that, like most men in Harmony, his father was suspicious of counseling or any other endeavor that might suggest a personal weakness.

"Psychiatrists? What do they know? They'll set me down on a couch and ask me if my father ever spanked me, then charge me two hundred dollars. Of course my father spanked me. And it's a good thing he did, or no tellin' how I'd have turned out. Problem today is that fathers reason with their children, talk till they're blue in the face. I say spank their heinies until they walk the straight and narrow, just like my dad did with me. And you're not too old for me to do that to you, Sam, so watch yourself."

Sam came back inside the house, just as his father came across the *Dr. Tom Show* while flipping through the television channels. Four men were seated in a circle talking about male menopause and getting in touch with their manhood.

"For crying out loud, would you listen to that. What's so hard about being a man? You work, take care of your family, see that your kids learn respect, and get your wife something at Christmas. What's so hard about that?" Charlie said.

"I liked what Dr. Tom said about men needing to be more open, that they don't always share their feelings," Gloria said. "Maybe you'd feel better if you talked to someone about how you feel."

"What's wrong with the way I feel? I just had my chest sawed open. How am I supposed to feel? Happy? My son wants to ship me off to the nuthouse, and you expect me to be Mr. Sunshine."

Sam didn't think his mom would likely raise the subject again.

To Sam's disappointment, the meeting seemed to be thriving in his absence. Krista Riley had delivered three sermons, to rave reviews. Bea Majors had cornered him in the produce department at the Kroger and extolled Krista's many virtues.

"Sam, she opens her mouth, and the Lord starts speaking through her. You know how you preach from notes? Well, she doesn't. She just stands up there and speaks from her heart. Oh, and her prayers are beautiful. I feel like I'm transported to heaven just listening to her."

"That's wonderful," Sam said. "I'm glad you're enjoying her."

"So when did you say you'd be back?"

"In two months."

"That soon?" Bea said, clearly disappointed by the brevity of Sam's absence.

"So how's everyone doing?" Sam asked.

"Real well. You know how Fern has warts real bad?"

"Yes."

"Krista went to visit and laid hands on her, said a prayer, and all the warts went away. Every last one of them."

"Well, that's wonderful," Sam said. "Tell Fern I'm happy for her."

"That's not all. Stanley Farlow won fifty dollars in the lottery. I tell you, Sam, ever since she's come, we've been blessed."

"It sounds as if the Lord is doing some wonderful things through her."

"Everybody likes her," Bea went on. "She got four invitations to dinner this past Sunday."

Sam hadn't received four invitations to dinner in his six years at Harmony Friends.

"And the kids just love her. She's started a kids' program and had twenty-three children the first night."

"I couldn't be happier," Sam said, now thoroughly miserable.

"The old people like her too. She's already been to the nursing home four times. And last week she gave a program at the Senior Center. She played the guitar and had everybody singing. She knows all the old songs."

"That's wonderful."

"How's your father?"

"Oh, he's hanging in there. He's awful sore still and rather grumpy."

"Maybe Krista could come over and pray for him," Bea suggested.

"Yes, well, perhaps I'll call her."

"I'm sure she'd be happy to do it. She seems to have a real heart for ministry."

Bea appeared to have much more to say, but Sam excused himself. "Like to stay and chat, but I promised Barbara I'd be right home."

He rounded the corner to the frozen foods, and there stood Dale Hinshaw, surveying the ice cream. Sam tried ducking behind a display of soda pop, but wasn't quick enough.

"Hold on there, Sam. Need to talk with you."

"Oh, hi, Dale. What's up?"

"It's about that woman pastor you sent away for."

"I didn't send away for anybody. The meeting did."

"Well, whoever did got us a witch."

"A witch? You mean she's grouchy?"

"No, I mean she's a witch. She lights a candle at the start of worship. It's witchcraft, plain and simple. And you know what the Bible says about witches. It's a work of the flesh, an abomination to the Lord."

"I'm sure it is. I just don't see how lighting a candle has anything to do with being a witch."

"She's conjuring up evil spirits," Dale said. "You see any movie on television about witches, and the first thing they do is light a candle."

"Is that so?"

"It sure is. Now what are you going to do about it?"

"I'm going to take care of my father."

Dale snorted. "That's a fine how-do-you-do. Our church is being taken over by witches, and you're worried about your father."

Standing in the frozen foods, it occurred to Sam that pastoring in a small town, although in some ways advantageous, was also distressing. A simple trip to the grocery store was fraught with peril, a veritable landmine of ecclesial warfare.

He didn't answer Dale, who stood slack-jawed, staring at Sam as he pushed his cart down the aisle toward the checkout counter, deep in thought. Mostly he thought about the other pastors he'd known, how so many of them had left the ministry weary and disillusioned.

Waiting in line, he tried to remember what it was he liked about being a pastor. He enjoyed being around people. Well, most people anyway. There were moments of pure holy radiance, when he felt transported. Though rare, those times nourished him. The pastorate was a ringside seat to life. He worried that, were he to leave it, he'd no longer witness such glories—weddings, reconciliations, and even funerals, when in the confidence of faith a sorrow was changed to joy.

He wouldn't miss the board meetings.

"Earth to Sam."

Startled, he looked up.

"Is that everything?" Sally Fleming asked, standing at the cash register.

"Oh, sure. Yes, sorry. How are you, Sally?"

"I'm fine. You looked awful deep in thought."

"Just daydreaming is all."

"We miss you at church," Sally said. "When are you coming back?"

"Two more months. How are Wayne and the children?"

"They're all well."

"Good, good. Give them my greetings."

"Give my best to Barbara and the boys. And your parents too."

"Will do, Sally. Good seeing you."

Sam collected his bag at the end of the counter and walked the three blocks home, pausing to visit with Uly Grant at the hardware store.

"How's your new boarder?" Sam asked.

"Very quiet. She's hardly ever here, except to sleep. Mostly she's out visiting folks or over at the meetinghouse."

Sam had been a teenager the last time he'd seen the upstairs apartment and was hoping for a tour. "So what's it like up there?"

"Real nice. We put new carpet in, a new kitchen and bathroom and draperies and wallpaper. Pretty well had to gut the whole place and start over."

"It was awful nice of you to donate it to the church."

"It's just the three months," Uly said. "Probably better to have someone living in there anyway."

"I haven't been up there in years. Not since we were kids."

"Would you like to see it, Sam?"

"Sure."

"Well, stop by then when Krista's here. I'm sure she'd be happy to show you around."

The problem with Uly Grant was that he couldn't take a hint.

"Did you hear the Darnells have started coming back?" Uly asked.

The Harry Darnell family had left in a huff in 1949 after losing a scorching debate over the proper color for pew cushions.

"You're kidding? The Darnells?"

"Yep, Krista went to visit them and they came back. 'Course Harry's dead, but all his kids and grandkids showed up. We had to set out extra chairs."

"I thought they were Methodists."

"That's where they attended, but it turns out they never joined. Said they'd just been waiting all these years for the Quakers to invite them back."

"Well, I'll be. Imagine that."

"Good thing Krista thought to visit them."

"Yes, it was."

"She has a real pastor's heart," Uly said.

"That's what I've heard."

"She cured Fern Hampton of her warts."

"Amazing," Sam said. "Simply amazing."

"Not that we don't miss you, Sam. We'll be glad to have you back." He clapped Sam on the back. "By the way, how's your dad?"

"Coming along, but he still needs quite a bit of help."

"It's a good thing you can be with him."

"Yes, I feel fortunate. And I'm glad the meeting is in such capable hands."

"It sure is that. She's a dandy. My boys love her."

Sam pushed back a rising tide of envy.

"Good to see you, Uly. You take care."

"See you," Uly said cheerfully. A little too cheerfully to suit Sam.

He passed his family on the way home. Barbara leaned out the car window. "We're going to the meetinghouse. Want to come?"

"What's going on there?"

"Didn't you hear, Dad?" Levi piped up from the backseat. "Krista's having a party for the kids. She's really neat. I like her. Why didn't you ever have a party for us?"

Now his own children were turning on him.

In the next two blocks, three church members stopped him to yammer about what a breath of fresh air Krista Riley was, enumerating her many virtues and looking disappointed at the prospect of his return.

Arriving home, he checked the answering machine. There were no messages for him—there hadn't been for days—so he retired to the hammock in the backyard to read a book.

Preoccupied with his fading popularity, Sam couldn't concentrate. His mistake, he realized now, was in not picking his own replacement. He should have recommended they hire the superintendent's nephew, a toad of a man, who would have so annoyed the congregation they'd have welcomed Sam's return with open arms and a raise. Instead, they'd chosen someone with initiative who made Sam look like a slacker, someone who was silk to his burlap.

Doesn't that take the cake, he thought miserably. I work my caboose off for six years, then they throw me over for a pretty face. That's gratitude for you! He swung in the hammock, contemplating the sorry end of his career.

fourteen

The First Tremor

The morning of the Corn and Sausage Days parade found Sam Gardner seated in the back of Ellis Hodge's Ford pickup truck, a *Grand Marshal* sign taped to the driver's door, with Ellis at the wheel. The process of Sam's being named grand marshal was a circuitous one, having begun the evening before when Harvey Muldock had phoned to report that their state representative, the Honorable Henry Tuttle, had been stricken with the flu.

Sam was sympathetic and asked Harvey if he should send a get-well card, even though he hadn't voted for Henry Tuttle and had only met him once, when the Honorable Mr. Tuttle had shaken his hand and called him Jim.

"Send him a card if you want," Harvey said. "That's your business. But he was supposed to be our grand marshal, and now he's sick. Who can we get to replace him?"

"How about Clevis Nagle?" Sam suggested. "He's done a lot of good for the town."

"He was grand marshal year before last."

"Well, then, how about Mabel Morrison?"

"Too grouchy. She wouldn't wave at people."

"Yeah, you're probably right. How about you being our grand marshal, Harvey?"

"Can't. I'm driving the Sausage Queen."

"Oh, that's right."

Sam wracked his brain, trying to think of someone who would look dignified in the back of Ellis Hodge's pickup truck. "Say, how about Dr. Pierce? He's a good guy."

"Already tried him. He has to work."

It was apparent they would have to settle for a lower-echelon grand marshal.

"Bob Miles?" Sam suggested.

"If Bob does it, there won't be anyone to take pictures."

"Good point. Didn't think of that. Hey, how about Fern Hampton's nephew, Ervin. He's been doing a great job with the manhole covers."

"Nope, he's working security."

"Security? What security?"

"You know that money we got from the federal government for homeland security?"

"Yes," Sam said.

"We used it to pay Ervin to check the sewer system for bombs the day of the parade. He can't do that and be the grand marshal."

"No, I suspect not."

"How about you be the grand marshal, Sam?"

"Me?"

"Yeah, you'd be a fine grand marshal."

"Well, I suppose I could, if you think it'd help."

Even though he'd been the seventh choice, Sam felt honored, though the tribute was a bit tarnished when he arrived at the parade to find Ellis kneeling by the sign taped to his truck, felt-tip pen in hand, crossing out Henry Tuttle's name and writing *Sam Gardner* just above it.

Sam climbed in the rear of the pickup and situated himself in the lawn chair Harvey had advised him to bring, as the bed of the truck was littered with straw and cow manure. Sporting a new shirt and a fresh haircut—Kyle had opened his barbershop a half hour early to groom Sam in a manner befitting a grand marshal—Sam wished Ellis had been as particular. The truck was streaked with mud. Ellis Hodge had agreed three months before to be in the parade, but gave the appearance of having just been drafted to perform the service.

"Sorry about the mess, Sam. Meant to hose off the truck, but time got away from me."

"Yes, well, that can happen."

Ellis studied the slip of paper. "Looks like they got us right after the high-school band and just before Johnny Mackey and his hearse."

"I thought the grand marshal was supposed to be at the head of the parade."

Ellis peered at the list. "Nope. Sausage Queen first, then the Odd Fellows, followed by the Shriners on their minibikes and the band, then us."

"Who follows us?"

"Let me see, we got the Little League teams, and the Baptists have a float, and Uly Grant on his mower and the fire department, then the past Sausage Queens."

This encompassed nearly the entire population of the town, leaving scarcely anyone to watch, except the parents of the Sausage Queen, who were seated with other dignitaries on the balcony above the hardware store overlooking the parade route.

The night before, Buffy Newhart had been chosen the Sausage Queen, bequeathed the Sausage Scepter, crowned with the Sausage Tiara—pure stainless steel adorned with a hundred rhinestones in the shape of sausage patties and links—and had her picture taken for inclusion on the Sausage Queen Wall of Fame at the Odd Fellows Lodge. For the past three years, Buffy had aspired to royalty but had never been able to overcome her greatest defect—an overbite of beaverlike proportions. But this past year, she had given the judges something else to notice by having certain features of her body surgically enhanced, which had the desired effect. As Sam watched from the back of Ellis's truck, he thought Harvey Muldock seemed especially attentive as he took Buffy by the elbow and helped her into his 1951 Plymouth Cranbrook convertible. He wondered how Harvey's heart could stand the excitement of being in close proximity to Buffy Newhart. Then again, he thought, if Harvey did succumb, collapsing of a heart attack in the lovely arms of Buffy Newhart in his beloved Cranbrook convertible was a glorious way to go.

At precisely eleven o'clock, Harvey tooted his horn, turned the key, and bumped the gearshift down three notches to drive. The transmission clunked into place, the Cranbrook lurched ahead, causing Buffy to pitch forward, a not uncommon occurrence with someone whose ballast had been medically rearranged. By the time they reached the hardware store she'd recovered nicely and with the charm befitting a Sausage Queen was waving to her adoring subjects.

Three weeks into her new vocation, Krista Riley was tired but generally pleased with the direction of her life. Her classes were stimulating, stretching her mind and spirit; her ministry at Harmony Friends was, to put it mildly, interesting. Her preaching had been well received by the congregation, with the exception of Dale Hinshaw, who'd accused her of several transgressions, including witchcraft, blasphemy, and voodoo.

Frank, the church secretary, was proving to be an invaluable aide, as was Miriam Hodge, who ran interference against Dale, keeping him at bay, except for an occasional telephone recording at various hours of the day urging her to attend Harmony Friends Meeting and get right with the Lord.

Fern Hampton, despite being healed of her warts, was still aloof. When Krista had volunteered to help make noodles for the Friendly Women's Circle annual Chicken Noodle Dinner, Fern had loftily informed her that noodle making was something one aspired to, a rank to be attained after years of service by women whose moral character was beyond reproach.

Bea Majors had intervened, pointing out that Krista was a minister, but Fern had held fast. "Minister or not, we've known her less than a month. What if she turns out to be a fraud? There goes our reputation. She can make tea, but she doesn't touch the noodles."

The morning of the Corn and Sausage Days parade, Krista was bustling around her apartment, readying herself for the grand event, when she heard a knock on her door. She opened it to find a man and woman with unusually prominent teeth and carrying lawn chairs, standing in the hallway.

"We're the Newharts," they said, entering her apartment. "Perhaps you know our daughter, Buffy."

"I haven't had the pleasure."

"She's this year's Sausage Queen."

"That's wonderful. I'm sure you're quite proud of her," Krista said pleasantly.

"We certainly are that."

They were standing in the middle of Krista's living room by now.

"Don't mind us," they said. "We'll just take our seats on the balcony."

"Excuse me?"

"The balcony. The parents of the Sausage Queen get to sit there, along with the members of the town council."

No one had mentioned this to Krista, though she was starting to realize she'd been uninformed about many of Harmony's more curious customs.

"Help yourself," she said. "I'm off to the meetinghouse. If you use the bathroom, be sure to jiggle the toilet handle."

"Will do," they said.

She was late, so she hurried, the faint strains of parade music pulling her along.

When she arrived at the meetinghouse, Fern was waiting at the door, a frown on her face, peering at her wristwatch. "You're an hour late," she snapped.

"Sorry, Fern. I had to finish my schoolwork."

"Don't let it happen again," Fern said, then handed her an index card. "This is the recipe for the iced tea. Follow it precisely."

Krista began boiling water for the tea, then added the tea bags to let it steep, giving it an occasional stir. Fern peered over her shoulder the entire time, cautioning her to slow down. "Careful, careful. That's tea you're making, not a milk shake."

As in most dictatorships, Fern's subjects were too cowed to intervene and busied themselves with other tasks, lest they draw her attention and then her wrath.

Fern was momentarily distracted when Opal Majors dropped a bowl of ice cubes and Krista, in sheer defiance of the recipe, used the opportunity to add a tablespoon of sugar to the tea.

Fern turned around just in time to see Krista set the sugar bowl on the counter.

"What did you just do? You just did something. What was it?" she demanded.

"The tea tasted bitter. I thought a little sugar might take the edge off."

"Pour it out. You've ruined it," Fern ordered, then turned to Bea. "This is exactly what I warned you about. First she was late, and now she's changing things." She turned back to confront Krista. "We never put sugar in the tea. We have sugar packets. One per customer. Now you've gone and ruined everything. Pour it out. It's no good now."

"Fern, that would be wasteful," Krista said. "It's perfectly good tea." Fern gasped, clearly not accustomed to having her orders ignored. The other women fell silent, glancing warily at the unfolding drama, like a herd of sheep whose most vulnerable member was being singled out by a wolf.

"Out!" Fern demanded, drawing herself up to full height, jutting her chest out, and pointing to the door. "Out of the kitchen! I knew this would happen."

Krista began to laugh and said, "Oh, Fern, relax! As my students used to say, 'Chill out!'"

Miriam Hodge, apparently emboldened by Krista's bravery, tittered. Then Bea Majors tried to stifle a snort but failed, and finally all the other Friendly Women began cackling like crazed hens.

"Hush!" Fern screeched, which caused the women to laugh even harder.

Dictators can suppress individual acts of defiance, but collective mutiny is not as easily squashed, and laughter in the face of tyranny is an especially potent weapon.

"Enough of this insubordination," Fern snapped. "I won't have it."

"Oh, Fern, settle down," Opal Majors said.

For over sixty years, the Hampton women had ruled the Friendly Women's Circle with an iron fist, crushing dissent lest it give birth to liberation. Their chief weapons had been gossip and slander, but when those failed to subdue, martial law was never far behind.

"That's it, no Chicken Noodle Dinner this year," Fern said. "We're shutting it down."

"What do you mean, we're shutting it down?" Jessie Peacock said. "We can't do that. People will be here within the hour. We've cooked all these noodles. We even advertised in the *Herald*."

"Then you'll have to choose. It's either her or me. But if you pick her, I'm taking the noodle cutters with me."

The women waited a few seconds before answering to give Fern the impression they were considering her ultimatum, then Bea said, rather timidly, "Fern, she is our pastor . . ."

With that, Fern Hampton harrumphed, collected the noodle cutters, and stormed from the kitchen, vowing aloud that Krista Riley's time at Harmony Friends Meeting would soon be coming to an end.

Jessie Peacock was the first to recover. "It'd serve her right if her warts came back."

"Don't you worry, honey," Miriam Hodge said, hugging Krista. "She's always like this on Chicken Noodle Day."

"What do you mean? She's like this every day," Bea Majors said.

"Fern seems really upset. Maybe I should go apologize and ask her to come back," Krista said.

"Let's quit while we're ahead," Bea said.

The women returned to their labors, and Krista joined them, appreciative of their support, but suspecting a bull's-eye had been planted firmly on her back and that Fern Hampton was practicing her aim.

Fifteen

A Miracle, Sort Of

*T*he Chicken Noodle Dinner was a stunning triumph, owing to Buffy Newhart's plug at the end of the parade in an interview with Bob Miles of the *Herald.*

"What are you doing next?" he'd asked her. "What are your plans for the future?"

"I'm going to the Chicken Noodle Dinner," she'd said.

Over the years many a Sausage Queen has been confounded about what to do after the glory of queenship. A few moved on to further glories, most notably Nora Nagle, who starred as a dancing grape in an underwear commercial. But many more struggled, having peaked early. It is the unspoken shame of Harmony that of the forty-two former Sausage Queens, fifteen of them required psychiatric treatment, twelve moved to the city, five of them took to drink, and one became a Buddhist.

Still, young ladies all over town aspire to that high office, knowing it might spell their ruination; they seem to be willing to risk their future in hopes of achieving that fleeting honor.

As was the custom, the freshly crowned Sausage Queen Buffy Newhart gave the blessing of the noodles, thanking God for first one thing and then another—the privilege of representing the town at the state Sausage Queen contest, the food they were about to partake of and the hands that had prepared it, and the opportunity to live in a free country where they could worship anywhere they wished or not worship at all, if that was their choice, amen.

Dale Hinshaw was pleased until she hit the last line, when he became visibly upset, having labored for years to make worship mandatory, lobbying the Honorable Henry Tuttle to sponsor a bill requiring every citizen to worship each Sunday, ideally at a Protestant church, unless one couldn't be found, then at a Catholic church, so long as one didn't make a habit of it.

He wanted to admonish Buffy but couldn't get near her for the entourage that surrounded her, attending to her every wish. Instead, he recorded her transgression in his pocket notebook, lest he forget her sin amidst the rapture of noodles and general excitement.

With Fern Hampton gone, Krista Riley served the noodles, spilling not one noodle the entire afternoon. This was akin to pitching a no-hitter her first time on the mound, and when she laid down her spoon two hours later, the Friendly Women broke into applause.

Sam's entire family was present in the meetinghouse basement, including his brother, Roger, who'd driven out from
the city for the day.

It was Charlie Gardner's first foray into public since his
heart bypass, and he was stuffing himself with noodles.

"Best noodles anywhere," Charlie Gardner said, scraping
his plate with a flourish.

His wife beamed with pleasure.

Krista, moving from table to table to chat with the lingering
diners, approached Sam's table. "How are the Gardners?"

"Finer than a frog's hair," Charlie Gardner said, his mood
elevated by the surfeit of noodles.

"I'm Roger," Sam's brother said, standing up and smiling
broadly, his bachelor radar on high alert in the presence of an
attractive single woman.

"It's a pleasure to meet you, Roger," Krista said, shaking
his hand.

"Please join us," he offered, holding out an empty chair
conveniently located beside his.

"I'd like nothing more," she said. "But there's still a lot of
work to be done."

"Oh, rest for a spell," Gloria Gardner said. "You've earned
it." She turned and spoke to Sam. "You wouldn't believe how
hard Krista's worked. I don't know what we would have done
without her."

"Better watch out, son. She might take your job," Charlie
Gardner teased.

"You know us women, we're sneaky that way," Krista said, poking Sam's shoulder.

Sam frowned. A look of alarm crossed his face.

"So how do you like being a minister so far?" Gloria Gardner asked.

"I'm having a ball," Krista said. "But, Sam, I don't know how you do it. Every time I turn around, there's something else to do. They told me you've been pastoring eighteen years now. How have you lasted so long?"

Sam smiled modestly, started to speak, but was interrupted by his father.

"He doesn't work very hard, that's how he does it," Charlie Gardner said. "Frank does most of the work."

That's the last time I buy him Cheetos and Dr. Pepper, Sam thought.

"So how do you find time for your boyfriend?" Roger asked Krista. Roger was still single, fast approaching forty, and had lost all sense of subtlety.

"Easy," Krista said. "I don't have one."

"If I've told Sam this once, I've told him a hundred times, don't be so busy with your career that you forget to love."

Sam rolled his eyes. Roger had never told him any such thing.

Krista blushed and began gathering empty plates onto a tray to carry to the kitchen.

"Let me help you," Roger offered, ever the gentleman.

"Somebody better hose him down," Sam whispered to Barbara, who snorted, then began to laugh.

In the midst of her laughter Sam glanced across the table at his father, who was holding his chest, his face the color of a radish.

"Dad, you okay?" Sam asked.

"My chest," his father gasped.

Sam turned to his mother. "Call for an ambulance. Quick."

He ran around the table to his father and helped him to the floor, loosening his shirt collar.

The Friendly Women gathered around, concerned, their hands clutched in prayer.

"Dad, where does it hurt?" Sam asked.

"Chest ... arm ... neck," his dad answered weakly.

"Oh, Lord, he's having a heart attack," Bea Majors said. "Lift his legs. If someone's having a heart attack, you need to lift their legs."

"That's if they're having a stroke," Jessie Peacock said.

"No, Bea's right," Opal Majors said. "You got to lift their legs."

Jessie Peacock, always one for compromise, said, "How about just lifting one of his legs."

"C-c-cold," Charlie Gardner chattered.

"Barbara, run and get the blanket from our car," Sam said.

"Probably heartburn from all those noodles," Opal said, then absolved herself of any blame. "I told him not to eat so many. He had three plates."

Gloria Gardner returned to her husband's side, crouching on the floor beside him to smooth his hair and comfort him. "Johnny Mackey's on the way. You just hold on, honey."

The uninitiated might rest easy to learn an ambulance was on its way, but those familiar with Johnny Mackey's history of procrastination were not at all comforted by Gloria's report. Johnny had been known to stop for gas, groceries, and even lunch on his way to a medical emergency.

Barbara bustled in, carrying a blanket, which Sam spread over his father.

Dale Hinshaw knelt beside Charlie. "Times like this, a man needs to get right with the Almighty. You got any sins to confess before you meet the Lord?"

"Dale, don't you have somewhere else to be?" Sam asked, gently nudging him aside.

"Adultery? Lying? Cheating? Anything at all you need to repent of?" Dale persisted, oblivious to Sam's hint.

Some men dream of illicit romance, others of vast fortunes. It seemed Dale Hinshaw had long fantasized of leading a dying sinner to the Lord. Unfortunately, Charlie Gardner wasn't cooperating.

"How about drinking? Stealing? Did you ever murder anyone?"

Charlie shook his head, albeit feebly.

"Lust? Greed? Gluttony?" Dale pressed on.

"He's got you there, Charlie," Opal Majors said. "Three plates of noodles. If that isn't gluttony, I don't know what is."

"Gluttony it is," Dale cried out gleefully. "I knew there was a demon in there somewhere. We just had to root him out."

The whole time Dale was working feverishly to exorcise

Charlie's demons, Krista stood with her arm around Gloria Gardner, unsure of what to do.

When Dale paused to catch his breath, she suggested they pray for Charlie, in hopes it would silence Dale.

"Good idea," Dale said and began to beseech the Lord to forgive Charlie for overindulging. "Lord, we ask your mercy here on Charlie, even though he's disobeyed your Word and made a pig of himself—"

"Actually," Krista interrupted, "I was hoping we could have Quaker silence."

"Pipe down, Dale," Bea Majors said, then turned to Krista. "Since you cured Fern of her warts, why don't you have a go at Charlie."

Krista knelt, laid her right hand upon Charlie's chest, and began to pray quietly. People pressed in, straining to hear, but her voice was so soft they couldn't make out the words.

"For crying out loud," Dale groused. "I can't hear a word she's saying."

"Zip it, Dale. She's not praying to you," Bea Majors said.

At that precise moment, as if to punctuate Bea's counsel, Charles Gardner emitted the loudest, longest belch that had ever been heard in the environs of Harmony.

"Well, Dale, looks like he expelled that demon you were talking about," Bea Majors observed.

Charlie's eyes fluttered open, and he sat up. "What's everybody doing looking at me?" he asked. "Hey, what am I doing on the floor?"

Opal Majors, though not of the Roman persuasion, crossed herself. "My Lord, she's done it again. First, she cured Fern, then she didn't spill a noodle, and now she's gone and healed Charlie. We got ourselves a miracle worker."

The Friendly Women studied Krista silently, not certain what to make of such powers and the woman who held them.

Sam stepped back away from the crowd and regarded Krista quietly, torn between deep appreciation for her ministry and a rising envy for her gifts.

Sixteen

Dark Days

J ohnny Mackey arrived at the meetinghouse an hour later. Charlie was working on a fourth plate of noodles to build his strength, Gloria was washing dishes, Sam and Barbara and their sons were mopping the floor, and Roger was glued to Krista's side, tighter than a tick.

"Sorry I'm late," Johnny said. "Couldn't find my keys."

Over the years, Johnny Mackey's ambulance keys had been found in a number of interesting locations, including the counter of the Coffee Cup. Frank had hung them on the bulletin board in hopes someone might claim them, which Johnny did a month later, though not before transporting the sick and lame in the bed of his pickup.

"It's all right," Sam told Johnny. "Dad's better now." He had to bite his tongue to keep from stating the obvious—that with Johnny Mackey manning the ambulance, it behooved the populace to pray for divine intervention.

"Say, those noodles sure look good," Johnny said. "Got any left?"

"Help yourself," Charlie said as he served himself his fifth plate.

"So how you feeling?" Johnny asked, in between bites of noodles.

"Terrific. It was the craziest thing. One minute, my chest is killing me, and I'm stretched out on the floor thinking I'm gonna die. The next minute I'm feeling tip-top."

"What happened?" Johnny asked.

"Don't know and can't remember. Gloria said Krista laid her hand on my chest, said a prayer, and here I am. That little missy sure is something."

Sam was relieved when his father's description of Krista's many virtues was interrupted by a panting Bob Miles, camera slung around his neck, his notebook at the ready. He looked rather startled to see Charlie Gardner in the full bloom of health.

"I heard you were dead. I was going to take your picture for the *Herald.*"

"Sorry to disappoint you," Charlie said.

"What happened?"

Charlie's enthusiasm for his near-death experience was growing, and he recounted, with several dramatic embellishments, how Krista had, in his words, "plucked him from the jaws of death."

"What we need," Bob said, "is a photographic reconstruction. Charlie, you lie down there on the floor." He marched over to Krista and led her beside Charlie. "Krista, you kneel down and put your hand on Charlie's chest just like you did.

Then maybe if you could lift your other hand up to heaven, like you're commanding the Lord to heal Charlie. That'll add a little pizzazz."

Krista had severe misgivings, but Charlie was desperate to have his picture in the paper, so she went along, despite her better judgment.

"Now on the count of three, you both look at me and smile," Bob said.

"One, two, and think of your wedding night, three," Bob said, then clicked the shutter and smiled happily. "The Sausage Queen just got bumped to page two."

As he watched from across the basement, Sam felt prickly with envy—warm and flushed and slightly mad. Krista had been in Harmony a scant two months and she'd already cured Fern of warts, served on the front line of the Chicken Noodle Dinner, saved a life, and had her picture taken for the front page of the *Herald*.

It had taken him six years working the Chicken Noodle Dinner to be promoted to the lemonade line, and the best he'd done in the *Herald* was page four, when Bob had printed his and Barbara's engagement picture seventeen years before.

Even as he was consumed with resentment, he knew it was wrong but felt powerless to repent, so strong were his feelings. And when he left the meetinghouse an hour later, his family in tow, he was preoccupied with concern for his employment and more than a little grouchy, snapping at his family and being a general pain in the posterior the rest of the day.

A good night's rest restored his mood, and after breakfast Sam walked to his parents' house, where he found his father out in the garage, gassing up the lawn mower.

"Hi, Dad. Whatcha doing?"

"What's it look like I'm doing?"

"Filling the mower with gas," Sam ventured.

"You got it."

"If you need me to mow, I'll have to go back home and get my old tennis shoes," Sam said. "I don't want to get these grass-stained."

"Don't bother. I'll do the mowing."

Sam went inside, where he found his mother seated at the kitchen table, drinking a cup of coffee.

"Did you know Dad is going to mow?"

"Yes, he woke up this morning bound and determined to mow. I told him not to, that it was too soon after his operation, but he says he feels fine." She shook her head, exasperated. "Why don't you go out there and stop him?"

Sam chuckled. "Yeah, right. I'm sure he'll listen to me."

"What should we do?"

"Well, I think I'm going back to work," Sam said.

"I thought you had another month off," his mother said.

"I guess that's technically true. But since I took off to help with Dad and he's doing fine, I'm sure they'll be happy to have me back early. Besides, it'll save them from having to pay two pastors."

The Quakers, Sam had learned over the years, were never as excited as when they were saving money.

Coincidentally, the elders were meeting that night. Sam ate an early supper and arrived at the meetinghouse a little before seven, just as the elders were pulling into the parking lot.

Miriam Hodge opened the meeting with a devotional thought, offered a brief prayer, then welcomed Sam to their meeting. "So what brings you here this evening? We weren't expecting you, since you're still on leave."

"That's what I wanted to talk about," Sam said. "Dad's doing better, and I'm ready to come back to work."

His statement was greeted with silence as the elders glanced awkwardly at one another.

Miriam Hodge was the first to find her voice. "We're certainly glad your father is better, Sam."

"Yeah, Sam. That's great news," said Asa Peacock.

"Does this mean Krista has to go?" Bea Majors asked, clearly disappointed at the prospect.

"I thought you were supposed to be gone another month," Harvey Muldock said.

"I was," Sam said. "But now that my father is better, I thought I'd come back."

"Why don't you take another couple months off," Opal Majors suggested.

"Now there's a thought," Harvey Muldock said.

This wasn't going quite the way Sam had hoped.

"I just thought if I came back now, it'd save the meeting from having to pay two pastors," he said.

"Oh, it's not that much money," Bea Majors said. This from the woman who in 1976 had demanded the church switch from Kivett's Five and Dime toilet paper to Kroger toilet paper in order to save eleven cents, ultimately costing the meeting Ned Kivett's tithe. Now she was spending money like a drunken sailor.

"I hate to see us break our word to Krista," Asa Peacock said. "We told her we'd need her at least three months."

"It wouldn't be good to break our word," Miriam Hodge agreed.

"Besides, I was hoping she'd cure me of my arthritis," Bea said. "If we let her go now, I can kiss that good-bye."

"Maybe I could have a go at your arthritis," Sam said, growing desperate.

"Nothing personal, Sam," Bea said, "but I've been on the prayer list three years now, and all your praying hasn't done diddly-squat for my arthritis."

"Maybe I could pray for you now," Sam suggested.

He bowed his head, reached over to Bea, who was seated beside him, laid a hand on her gnarled, arthritic fingers, and began to pray for the Lord to heal Bea of her wretched malady. When he finished praying, Sam looked at her expectantly.

She wiggled her digits, then winced. "No good, Sam. I guess it's up to Krista now."

"It's just as I suspected," Opal Majors said. "The power's gone out of you. Why don't you take another couple months off and get right with the Lord."

"Couldn't hurt," Asa Peacock said.

"Of course, you'd still be on the payroll," Miriam Hodge added.

"I'm sure Krista wouldn't mind staying an extra month," Harvey Muldock said, visibly pleased by the possibility.

The longer Sam stayed at the meeting, the worse his predicament grew. He excused himself before they decided to get shed of him completely.

It took him ten minutes to walk home. By the time he arrived, he had worked himself into a lather.

"You won't believe what happened," he told his wife.

"What?"

"They the same as gave me my walking papers. I went there to tell them I was ready to come back to work, and they gave me an extra month off. It's clear they don't want me back."

"Sam Gardner, you are one odd duck," Barbara said. "You've been complaining for years that you're overworked and underpaid. Now they want to give you paid time off and you're upset."

"You like her too, don't you?" Sam said.

"Like who?"

"Krista. You like her sermons better than mine."

"Sam, jealously doesn't become you."

"Jealous? Who said I was jealous? I'm not jealous."

Barbara sighed.

"Yes, I enjoy her sermons. But I like yours too. I think the meeting is fortunate to have both of you."

"Now my own wife has turned against me," Sam muttered, stalking from the room.

He busied himself at his workbench in the garage, building a doghouse. Barbara readied the boys for bed, gave him an extra hour to cool off, then went outside to gauge his mood.

"What are you building?"

"A doghouse."

"Who for?" Barbara asked.

"Us."

"We don't have a dog."

"I thought we could get one. That way I'd have at least one member of this family who was loyal to me."

She clenched and unclenched her fists, fairly vibrating with anger. "I'm going to bed. If you want to stay outside and feel sorry for yourself, you can, but I don't have to sit around and watch."

"I guess that proves my point," Sam said. "I have a problem and you don't want to be around me. If you were a dog, you'd be happy to be with me."

"If I were a dog, I'd bite you." She turned, walked to the garage door, then stopped. "You coming to bed anytime soon?"

"Probably not. I want some time by myself."

"Okay, then. See you in the morning."

"Good night," Sam said.

"Night."

For early autumn, it was a steamy night. Sam raised the window over his workbench and looked down the alley just as Shirley Finchum walked past with her dog on a leash, making their evening rounds.

"Hi, Mrs. Finchum," Sam said, peering through the window screen.

She gave a slight jump. "You startled me, Sam."

"Sorry about that."

"What are you doing in there?" Shirley asked.

"Oh, just puttering around."

"How's your dad?"

"Much better, thank you."

"I heard the new pastor healed him," she said.

"I wouldn't go that far," Sam said. "All he had was indigestion."

"They're saying he was dead and she brought him back to life."

"You know how rumors get started," he said dismissively.

"I was talking with Jessie Peacock today at the grocery, and she mentioned how much they all like her."

Sam frowned.

"Well, just between you and me, I don't hold with woman ministers. You know what the Bible says about them, don't you?"

It baffled Sam why people felt obligated to quote the Bible to pastors, most of whom had read the Bible, some more than once.

"It says a woman shouldn't teach a man is what it says," Shirley continued.

"Yes, ma'am, it surely does."

The Bible also said disobedient children should be stoned to death, but Sam didn't point that out. These were dark days, he reckoned, so he would take his friends wherever he could find them.

Seventeen

Fern Strikes

ern Hampton stewed in her juices that week, waiting for Krista to phone and apologize for her outrageous behavior. But she heard not a word. Indeed, no one from the meeting had called to plead forgiveness, and each day that passed heightened her fury. That Friday, she gathered the official minutes of the Friendly Women's Circle from her basement and marched down to the meetinghouse, where she dumped them on Frank's desk.

"What are these?" Frank asked.

"The minutes from the Circle. I'm quitting the church."

She stepped back, her arms folded across her chest, glaring at Frank and savoring the moment.

At this point, she knew, he'd plead with her not to act hastily, to please reconsider, that they couldn't manage without her.

"I'll be sure to pass them along to the Circle," Frank said. "Is that all you wanted?"

Fern had been a member of Harmony Friends all her crabby life, and her parents before her, and it had come to this—dismissed as one would toss away a soiled tissue.

Frank glanced at his watch. "Lunchtime. Gotta go. Been nice seeing you, Fern."

With that, he was out the door, like a man fleeing a tornado's approach.

Fern slithered into the pastor's office to hiss at Krista, but it was deserted, not a soul in sight. Then she strode through the meetinghouse, room by room, collecting the artifacts her family had donated over the years—the Frieda Hampton Memorial Clock, The Fleeta Hampton Memorial Pulpit Bible, and the Fred Hampton Memorial Pulpit Chair, where Sam sat each Sunday, before that interloper had come along.

Sam had bellyached about the chair since his first year there. The back was carved in the shape of an eagle, its beak facing forward, jabbing him smack between his fourth and fifth vertebrae. But no other pastors had ever complained. Pastor Taylor had sat in that very chair each Sunday for thirty years with nary a whimper. Pastors these days are whiners, Fern thought. She hauled the clock, Bible, and chair to her car, lifted them into the trunk, then sped away, her tires flinging pebbles against the side of the meetinghouse.

Krista walked around the corner just as Fern was fleeing the meetinghouse. Ordinarily, she entered through the back door, but this time, following a peculiar hunch she couldn't quite explain, she went through the meeting room to the office, which was how she noticed the sacred treasures were missing.

Someone had stolen the church's Bible! The nerve! She hurried into the office and dialed the police department, where Myron Gillis, only three days on the job, was itching to make his first arrest. Though Myron had never been trained as a police officer, he had the benefit of needing a job the same time his uncle, Harvey Muldock, had been charged with the responsibility of hiring a new officer for the town.

Myron listened carefully as Krista described the car she'd seen speeding away from the meetinghouse. He thanked her, assured her the treasures would be safely returned, then dashed to his car to track down the desperado who'd masterminded this blasphemous act. He caught up with Fern on Main Street, at the stoplight in front of the *Harmony Herald* building. Bob Miles watched from the front window of his office. This was the juiciest bit of news he'd witnessed in some time—Fern Hampton busted by the police. He typed away as the drama unfolded outside the window.

Being new to the job, Myron Gillis hadn't developed a keen sense of proportional response. After finding the Bible, clock, and chair in Fern's trunk, he handcuffed and escorted her to the backseat of his cruiser for a ride to the police station for interrogation and possible torture for stealing the sacred artifacts of Christianity. He'd known Fern all his life, but it was always the ones you knew who turned out to be secret agents of terrorist regimes.

Bob considered intervening, then decided against it. Journalists, after all, were to report the news, not thrust themselves in the middle of it. Instead, he snapped a photograph of Fern being hauled away, then hurried to have the film developed at the Kroger, where Shirley Finchum's daughter saw the evidence of Fern's headfirst fall into disgrace and phoned her mother to report Fern's plight.

The problem with being Fern Hampton is that your reservoir of goodwill is so shallow no one is inclined to come to your aid. Fern was given one call, which she used to phone Bea Majors, who was busy in her flowerbeds and couldn't get there until the next day. In the meantime, Shirley was working the phones, informing the populace of Fern's felony, which was how Krista learned about it.

She arrived at the police station just as Officer Gillis was fingerprinting Fern to check for past offenses.

Krista asked him to release Fern. "I didn't know it was her," she explained. "We certainly don't want to press charges against one of our church members."

"She told me she'd quit the church," Myron said. "So now can I arrest her?"

"Please let her go," Krista said. "It was all a misunderstanding."

Myron frowned. "That don't take care of everything. I can drop the theft charges, but I still got her for assaulting a police officer. She kicked me in the shin and said us Gillises didn't have the sense to come in out of the rain."

"I'm sure she regrets that," Krista said.

"No I don't," Fern said. "I meant every word. I taught all the children in that family, and they were all dumber than doorknobs."

"How about just one night in jail?" Myron pleaded.

"Go ahead, lock me up," Fern said. "I've got nothing to live for anyway, now that I've been kicked out of the church."

"Fern, you've not been kicked out," Krista said, helping her from the chair.

"It's clear I'm not wanted. No one's phoned or stopped by to see me."

"I'm sorry, Fern. I had no idea you were this upset."

"Well, you should have known. You're a minister, after all. You should know what I'm thinking."

Though Krista had only been pastoring two months, she had already observed a curious phenomenon—her parishioners were under the impression she was a mind reader, knew what they felt, knew when they were sick, indeed knew all manner of trivia about them without their ever telling her.

"I don't know what you're thinking, Fern. You should have called to tell me you were upset, and I would have visited you and we would have talked."

"Go ahead, blame it on me. I knew you would."

"I'm not blaming anyone. We parted company under difficult circumstances, and I thought it wise to give you time to cool off."

"So you knew I was mad and didn't do a thing about it," Fern said. "Some minister you are."

With that, she gathered her purse, glared at Myron Gillis, harrumphed at Krista, and marched from the police station.

"Wish I could have put her in the slammer," Myron Gillis said.

"Wish I would have let you."

Krista rose early the next morning, spent several hours on reading assignments and a paper for school, then drove to Cartersburg to meet a childhood friend for lunch. It was a difficult hour. Her friend's mother had passed away the week before, and Krista spent much of the hour listening to her friend lay bare her suffering. Reaching across the table, Krista held her friend's hand.

Across the restaurant, obscured by a palm plant, Fern Hampton peered through the fronds, aghast at Krista's conduct. She'd gone to the Wal-Mart, then had stopped for lunch, inadvertently stumbling into a den of iniquity! If she hadn't seen it, she wouldn't have believed it. But who could deny it now? Krista Riley, seated in a public restaurant holding hands with another woman. Right out in the open, in front of God and everyone.

Fern scrunched down behind the palm plant so Krista wouldn't see her and watched until Krista and her friend rose to leave, when they embraced one another, said good-bye, and exchanged air kisses.

If that wasn't proof, Fern didn't know what was.

What was ordinarily a forty-minute drive home took Fern thirty-one minutes. Opal Majors was the first person she called. After swearing Opal to secrecy, which she did to ensure Opal's undivided attention, Fern revealed the sordid news that their church was being taken over by perverts.

Opal gasped. She'd heard of things like this happening in California but had never imagined it could happen in Harmony.

"There that chippy little pastor of ours was, sitting in a restaurant holding hands with another woman, right out in the open," Fern said. "People were staring at them and everything. I tell you, I never felt so sick in all my life. And to think she's our pastor."

"Holding hands doesn't mean anything," Opal said.

"Then what about hugging and kissing. I suppose that was nothing."

"They kissed?"

"Right there in the restaurant, slobbering all over one another."

"Oh, my."

"And to think I let her hold my hands when she prayed for my warts," Fern said, with a shudder of disgust.

"Oh Lord, I just thought of something."

"What?"

"She's going over to Bea's this afternoon to pray for her arthritis. No telling what she'll do to Bea. I better warn her."

"You call Bea then. I'm calling Dale Hinshaw to tell him. He'll know what to do."

That Fern Hampton would judge Dale Hinshaw a reliable guide to anything was further proof of her addled mind.

"I thought you wanted to keep this a secret," Opal said.

"This is no time to keep silent. We got to warn people," Fern declared.

"I sure can't believe that of Krista. She seemed so nice."

"I saw it with my own eyes," Fern said. "I'm not making it up."

"I know, I know. It's just a shock."

"Well, I'm not surprised. There was something about that little missy that didn't feel right from the start."

"I kind of liked her myself," Opal said, then clarified, "Not in that way, of course. I just meant that she seemed nice."

"It's the nice ones you got to worry about. They're always hiding something. You'd better call Bea and tell her to lock her doors."

After hanging up, Fern phoned Dale.

"I knew it," he exclaimed triumphantly. "I knew there was something there. So that's why she came here, to turn us into one of those fluffy churches."

"Seems clear enough to me," Fern said.

"That's how they do it," Dale said. "They come into a church, all nice and polite, then they start working on the children, and next thing you know, the kids are singing about global warming and you're taking up an offering for world peace."

"What can we do?"

"We tell the elders, that's what we do," Dale said. "We've got to nip this in the bud."

They began working the phone with a scorching intensity, calling the elders to demand they meet and stamp out this abomination, lest the Lord, in His righteous anger, smite them all.

Eighteen

The Divide Deepens

K rista was working on her sermon that evening when she heard the elders come in through the back door and assemble in the meetinghouse basement.

"Oh, is there a meeting?" she asked Miriam. "I didn't see it on my calendar. It's a good thing I was here."

"It's you we're meeting about," Fern sniffed. "You thought you could keep your dirty little secret all to yourself, didn't you?"

"Fern, be kind," Miriam said.

"What's going on?" Krista asked.

"As if you don't know," Fern said.

"Krista, I'm sorry," Miriam said, "but Fern and Dale called a special meeting, so we have to have it. I'm sure it's all a misunderstanding."

"If you ask me, we can't be rid of her soon enough," Fern said.

"I'm not going to have you attend," Miriam said to Krista. "We'll meet. Then if it merits meeting with you, we'll set up a time to talk with you."

"Surely you're not going to let her preach tomorrow?" Fern said.

"Yes, she is," Miriam said. "She's our pastor, and she'll be bringing the message tomorrow."

"Well, that's a fine how-do-you-do."

Miriam walked Krista back to the office. "Don't you worry about anything. Fern's still upset about the Chicken Noodle Dinner, and she's found a way to get back at you."

"You sure I don't need to stay?" Krista asked anxiously.

"Let's not give Fern the satisfaction," Miriam said.

"All of this because I added sugar to the tea?"

"No, all of this because you didn't cower in her presence."

Krista finished writing her sermon, then walked to her apartment over the hardware store. For a Saturday night, it was unusually quiet. The lights from the Royal Theater flickered through the window into her living room. She'd thought of going to the movie, but after a day of sermon writing she was tired and more than a bit unsettled by Fern's animosity.

She was taking a class at seminary about church conflict. The professor talked in rosy tones about reasoning with people and finding common ground, but it was clear he'd never met anyone like Fern Hampton. Five minutes in the same room with Fern Hampton and he'd have her in a chokehold, squeezing for all he was worth.

She stretched out on the couch, closed her eyes, and envisioned a silent bulldozer grinding through her mind, pushing the unpleasantness away.

• • •

Back at the meetinghouse, Miriam Hodge listened carefully to Fern, wondering why she had ever volunteered in the church.

"So tell me again why you think Krista is a lesbian?" Miriam Hodge asked.

Fern shuddered. "Don't say that word. I hate it."

"If you're going to accuse someone of being one, then you should at least use the word," Miriam said. "It's not a bad word."

"You didn't see what I saw. It was terrible. She and that other woman were holding hands and hugging and kissing, right there in broad daylight."

"And from this, you've deduced that our pastor is a lesbian."

"I know one when I see one."

"Fern, when Amanda was in her car wreck last year, you gave me a hug. And you kissed me on the cheek. Does that mean you're a homosexual?"

"Don't be foolish. You know I'm not one of them."

"My point is that just because Krista hugged another woman doesn't mean she's a lesbian."

"It's all right here in the Scriptures," Dale Hinshaw piped up. "First chapter of Romans. Folks stop honoring God, next thing you know, women are committing shameless acts with one another. You can read about it in the Bible."

"Women committed shameless acts in the Bible?" Harvey Muldock asked, perking up. "How come Sam never preached on that?"

Miriam looked at Dale, perplexed. "What's that got to do with Krista?"

"Well, if you don't know, I can't tell you," Dale said.

"Where exactly in the Bible are these shameless women?" Harvey persisted, his interest in Scripture appearing to grow by the moment.

"As long as that woman is our pastor, I can't support this church financially," Fern said.

Typical Fern Hampton, Miriam thought. Fern donated precisely fifty-two dollars a year, tossing a wadded-up one-dollar bill in the offering plate each Sunday and doing that grudgingly, her pain in parting with her dollar obvious to anyone watching.

"You do what you need to do, Fern," Miriam said with a tired sigh.

"I'm going to follow the Bible," Fern said. "She sinned against me, threw me out of the kitchen the day of the Chicken Noodle Dinner. The Bible says I have to set her right."

"Fern's right," Dale said. "Matthew chapter 18, verse 15."

"And if she doesn't apologize, then I'll have to take some-one with me and talk with her again."

"You do that, Fern. You go talk to Krista," Miriam said. "Settle your differences with her, so we can get beyond this. It's hurting the church."

Krista woke to the sound of someone pounding on her door. She sat up on the couch, rubbed her eyes, and made her way across the room to open the door, where she saw Fern, who peered around Krista into the apartment. "Got anybody in there with you?"

"What brings you by at this hour?" Krista asked. "Would you like to come in?"

Fern stepped past Krista cautiously, as if she feared contagion.

"Would you care for a drink?" Krista offered, acting with a charity she didn't feel. "I think I have some lemonade."

"I didn't come to socialize. I'm here on the Lord's business. The church sent me."

"Oh, I see. Well then, please sit down and tell me what's on your mind."

Fern sat on the edge of the sofa, her back ramrod straight, clutching her purse as if she were afraid Krista would conk her on the noggin and steal it.

"Miriam Hodge sent me here to see if you're, uh, if you like women."

"Excuse me?"

"Miriam Hodge wants to know if you like women."

"Sure, I like women. Some of my best friends are women."

"That's not what I mean, and you know it! Don't think you can play dumb. I saw you holding hands and kissing that woman in the restaurant. Don't pretend you didn't."

"Fern, it's ten o'clock at night. I've had a long day, and I'm tired."

Fern took a deep breath, then jutted out her formidable bosom. "Miriam Hodge wants to know if you're a queer."

"Miriam Hodge wants to know what?" Krista asked, incredulous.

"She wants to know if you're queer," Fern repeated.

"I can't believe Miriam Hodge wants to know that," Krista said.

"She most certainly does. She said it was hurting the church and told me to come talk with you and get the matter settled."

Krista sat quietly, contemplating her response.

"Well, are you?" Fern asked.

"It isn't any of your business."

Fern gasped. "It most certainly is."

"I disagree, and I'm not going to answer," Krista said.

"That settles it. You must be one. Otherwise, you'd deny it."

"I'm not denying it," Krista said. "Nor am I affirming it. I simply won't dignify such an inappropriate question with an answer. My sexual orientation is none of the church's business."

Fern rose from the sofa. "You're our minister. Everything you do is our business." She marched across the room and as she exited the apartment said, "Since you won't be honest with me, I have no choice but to tell Miriam and the other elders you haven't cooperated."

When she got home, Fern phoned Dale Hinshaw, who was seated next to his phone, awaiting her report.

"It's just as we feared," Fern said, as if it pained her to reveal it. "She's queerer than a three-dollar bill."

"Did she admit it?"

"She didn't deny it."

"That settles it," Dale said. "The guilty ones never admit it."

"What do we do now?"

"Well, according to Matthew 18, you have to go back and take someone from the church with you. I'm happy to offer my expertise," Dale said humbly. "I've had some experience confronting backsliders."

"When should we speak with her?"

"How about we get to church early tomorrow, before Sunday school, and talk to her then?" Dale said. "That way, if she gets right with the Lord, she can go ahead and preach. And if she doesn't, I'll do the preaching."

"Dale, I fall to my knees each day and thank the Lord you're in our church. I don't know how we'd manage without you," Fern said, her voice catching.

The next morning Krista was seated at her desk, absorbed in her sermon, when Dale and Fern came into her office a half hour before Sunday school. They stood there several seconds, seemingly perturbed Krista didn't notice their august presence.

Dale cleared his throat.

Krista glanced up. Oh Lord, she thought, not these two. Not now.

"Good morning, Dale. Hello, Fern. What brings you here so early?"

"Concern for your soul," Dale said.

"Pardon me?"

"We're concerned for your soul," Fern said, though by the tone of her voice it was clear she didn't give a rat's patoot for Krista's soul or any other part of her.

"In obedience to Matthew 18, we've come to ask you to repent," Dale said.

"Repent for what?"

"You know what," Fern snapped.

"Is it true what Fern told me?" Dale asked.

"Probably not, but I can't say for sure since I don't know what she told you." Krista was starting to feel feisty.

"She told me you wouldn't answer her about whether or not you were homosexual."

"That's right," Krista said. "My sexual orientation is a private matter."

Dale tried to appear mournful, but even Krista, who hadn't known him long, suspected he was enjoying his role as inquisitor immensely.

"There's no use trying to hide it," Fern said. "I saw you and your little hussy yesterday in Cartersburg, making moon eyes at one another."

The start of Sunday school was fast approaching. Krista could hear people entering the meetinghouse. She rose from her chair and made her away to where Dale and Fern were standing.

"Are you two done?" she asked. "Or must I hear more of your nonsense?"

Dale began trembling in anger. "We'll be speaking to the church about this matter," he warned.

Krista pointed to the door. "Please leave."

"You can't talk to us this way," Fern blustered.

Years of teaching school had taught Krista how to handle the unruly. She grasped Fern's elbow in one hand and Dale's in the other, squeezed firmly in the soft spots, weakening their resistance, and escorted them to the door.

If ringside seats had been sold to the comeuppance of Dale and Fern, the church could have retired its debt and built a new wing, so weary were people of their bullying.

But Krista took no joy in what she had done and suspected that, rather than putting Dale and Fern in their proper place, she'd only succeeded in angering them further and would soon pay heavily for what she had done.

Nineteen

Sam the Weasel

S am Gardner sat with his wife, children, and parents in the fifth row on the right-hand side of the meetinghouse, directly behind Ellis Hodge and his assorted kin.

For the first eighteen years of his life, Sam had spent Sunday mornings staring at the back of Ellis's neck. Some people think of God when they hear a certain hymn, others when they read the Bible. Sam's thoughts turn to the Divine whenever he sees a farmer's neck.

Fern Hampton sat behind the Gardners. She was always stirred up about something, but this morning she seemed especially provoked. She fanned herself briskly with a Last Supper cardboard fan, compliments of the Mackey Funeral Parlor. When Krista appeared at the back door of the meeting room and made her way to the pulpit, Fern grew visibly agitated, fanning the air about her even more swiftly.

Sam leaned over and whispered in Barbara's ear, "I wonder what's got Fern all worked up?"

"Some act of human kindness, no doubt," Barbara whispered back.

They tittered until Sam's mother shushed them.

Bea Majors launched into a song on the organ, something Sam didn't recognize, which was not unusual. He couldn't identify most of the songs Bea played.

"What song is that?" he whispered to Barbara.

"'Amazing Grace.'"

"Are you sure it isn't 'Leaning on the Everlasting Arms'?" he whispered.

Barbara listened carefully. "'Bringing in the Sheaves,'" she said.

"Yes, that's it," Sam agreed.

That mystery solved, they leaned back in their pew, bowed their heads, and settled into the Quaker worship.

Bea's song shuddered to a merciful end, and she climbed down from the organ seat as one would dismount a stagecoach after a hard day's ride, flexing her back, stretching her arms, and wiggling her fingers.

Silence engulfed the room, though when Sam listened carefully he could hear the whisper of fabric as Fern fanned herself vigorously. Across the meeting room Harvey Muldock blew his nose with a loud honk, then inspected his handkerchief, clearly satisfied with the result.

"Is it almost over?" Sam's son Addison whispered, his head rolling back in boredom and thumping the pew. Barbara pulled him across her lap and rubbed his head, straightening his hair.

Sam glanced over at Dale Hinshaw, who was reading his Bible, his fingers tracing the words, his lips moving. Dale's favorite pastime was rummaging around the Old Testament in search of obscure rules someone might have broken, then standing during the Quaker silence each Sunday to pronounce judgment. Sam had been told that the week before Dale had accused Jessie Peacock of violating Deuteronomy 22:5 by wearing pants. When Asa had come to his wife's defense, Dale had declared, rather snootily, that he didn't value the opinion of a man who was in flagrant violation of Leviticus 19:9.

Krista had obviously learned from experience and stood to make the announcements before Dale could rise to rebuke a backslider.

For someone so new to ministry, Krista was unarguably polished. Where Sam ordinarily fumbled with the bulletin as he read the announcements, she recited them from memory, adding insightful commentary along the way.

Ralph Hodge came forward and announced the first hymn, which they sang poorly but with much zeal. Then Krista stood and invited people to share their joys and concerns. She listened carefully as others spoke, then ended with a prayer, lifting each person's name to the Lord.

Sam invariably forgot the names and had to end the joys-and-concerns prayer by saying, "We especially remember those whose names were mentioned." Everyone knew he'd already forgotten their names, and when he assured them after church, in the greeting line, that he'd pray for their loved ones, they were skeptical.

Barbara leaned over and whispered to Sam, "How does she do that?"

Sam snorted. "Oldest trick in the book. Anybody can do it. Just takes a little practice."

Miss Rudy, with the crisp enunciation of a librarian, read the Scripture, then returned to her seat next to Frank, who the month before, in defiance of pew protocol, had moved from the tenth row to the third row to sit with Miss Rudy, even though they weren't married. When people weren't talking about Krista, they were talking about them. As Miss Rudy made her way back to her seat, Dale frowned at her, clearly disturbed by her brazen behavior.

Krista preached about Jesus and the Pharisees. Sam could tell it was an effort for her not to name names. The sermon was brief, as fine preaching should be. When she finished, she sat down in a folding chair behind the pulpit. That's when Sam noticed the pastor's chair was missing. For that matter, so was the clock. What a delicious mystery that was! It gave him something to think about in the silence that followed.

The puzzle was solved when Fern Hampton rose in the quiet to speak. "Many of you have probably noticed the clock and Bible and pulpit chair are gone. The clock was given in honor of my sainted grandmother, and my own father made the chair." She paused dramatically, as if collecting herself. "I felt I had no choice but to take them after Krista threw me out of the church."

Across the meeting room, people gasped. Behind the pulpit, Krista shook her head.

Fern went on. "The truth is, our pastor is a wolf in sheep's clothing. I know some of you have been taken in by her so-called healings, but I knew from the start something wasn't right with her. This past Friday, she called the police and had me arrested for taking what was rightfully mine. Then yesterday she disgraced the church in public. I won't tell you what she did. It's too shameful to mention. But it had something to do with another woman. When I challenged her, she denied it. When I took Dale with me as a witness, she threw us out of the office."

Dale, looking appropriately saddened by the whole sordid matter, nodded solemnly.

"Sam has said he wants to come back, and I think it's high time we let him," Fern said. "That woman is tearing this church apart."

Sam perked up. He hoped others would stand and demand his return.

"Why do you care who our pastor is?" Frank said. "You told me on Friday you were quitting the church."

"I was mad with grief," Fern said. "I wasn't thinking right."

"This is wrong," Barbara whispered to Sam. "Stand up and say something."

Dale rose from his pew, stabbing the air with his finger to punctuate his words. "What we've got ourselves here is nothing but old-fashioned sin. Romans chapter 1, verse 26."

All over the meeting room, people reached for their Bibles. "Is that in the Old Testament or the New Testament?" Harvey Muldock asked.

Miriam Hodge stood. "This is inappropriate. Worship is not the time or place to accuse anyone of such things."

"The Bible is clear," Dale said. "Matthew 18. If someone in the church rejects correction from two persons, tell it to the church."

Barbara nudged Sam. "Say something," she said.

Sam knew it would be the honorable thing to do, but all he could think about was getting his job back, and he remained still.

"As the clerk of the meeting, I'm calling a special business meeting for this Friday evening at seven o'clock," Miriam said.

"Friday!" Harvey Muldock shrieked. "That's high-school football night. We can't meet on Friday."

"Friday night it is," Miriam declared firmly.

Harvey appeared genuinely torn, forced to choose between watching football or hearing about women committing unnatural acts. He groaned in anguish.

"Let us continue our worship in silence," Miriam said. "I ask you to pray that we might be gracious and wise, full of God's love for one another."

It was clearly too late for that.

After fifteen minutes of silence, Miriam rose and prayed, bringing the worship to a close. Krista walked down the center aisle, her head held high, stationing herself at the door to shake hands with people as they passed by, most of them averting their eyes.

Dale and Fern slunk out the side door.

Barbara didn't speak to Sam the whole way home. But when they were alone in their bedroom, she unloaded. "Sam Gardner, why didn't you say something? They said those awful things about her, and you didn't come to her defense."

"I didn't need to. Miriam did."

"You're the pastor. You should have said something."

"Technically, I'm not the pastor right now," Sam reminded her. "I'm still on leave."

"You weasel."

"Look, if Krista is going to be a pastor, she's going to have to deal with nutcases. The sooner she learns that, the better off she'll be."

"Maybe she wouldn't have to deal with nutcases if reasonable people found the courage to speak up," Barbara said.

"There's no talking with you when you get in this logical mood of yours," Sam said.

"Yes, I can see how logic might be hard to refute."

They'd had these arguments before, Barbara wanting Sam to take a firm stand and Sam refusing.

"I'm a pastor, not a prophet," he said. "Prophets get fired. Pastors have a family to support. Besides, I thought you believed in equality. You're perfectly free to stand up and defend Krista, if you wish."

"I might just do that. But I'll tell you something, Sam Gardner. Something I've never told you before. Something I never felt toward you before."

"What?"

"I'm losing my respect for you, that's what."

The room fell silent. Sam slipped off his dress clothes, hung them in the closet, then pulled on blue jeans and a sweatshirt.

"I'm doing this for you and the boys," Sam said finally. "Krista is gifted in ways I'm not, and people really like her. Don't you remember how we ended up back here? How my last church fired me because they liked that evangelist who came to speak? We had to move in with my folks, for crying out loud! I don't want to put you and the boys through that again."

"Don't hide behind us. We'd rather have a husband and father with character than one we don't respect."

"Yeah, Dad, it was pretty wienie of you not to stick up for Krista," Levi said from the other side of their bedroom door.

"Yeah, Dad, pretty wienie," Addison echoed.

"You boys stop listening to our private talks," Sam yelled. "And treat me with more respect."

"A wise person once told me respect couldn't be given; it had to be earned."

"Who told you that?"

"You did, Sam," Barbara said, walking from the room.

For crying out loud, he thought. They've all gone nuts.

Krista had planned on staying the afternoon in Harmony

visiting her flock, then driving back to the city in the evening. But it had taken all her energy and goodwill not to flee the meetinghouse after Miriam's prayer. Her appetite for fellowship was now considerably diminished. She stopped by her apartment, changed into her blue jeans, packed her suitcase, and began the long drive back to the city, wondering all the while if Principal Dutmire would hire her back.

She pulled into Ruth Marshal's driveway just before supper.

"I was hoping you'd return in time to join me," Ruth said, setting an extra plate on the table.

"I'm afraid I won't be good company tonight," Krista said.

Ruth Marshal had many fine qualities; one was an unerring instinct for when to listen. She turned off the stove, poured two glasses of iced tea, and sat at the kitchen table.

Krista told her everything—the tea in the sugar at the Chicken Noodle Dinner, Fern's brush with the law, her visits from Fern and Dale, wrapping up with a vivid description of that morning's worship.

Ruth Marshal said nothing at first. She took a sip of her tea, then leaned back in her chair, her brow creased in thought. After several moments, she leaned forward and said, "Do you want to know what I think?"

"Yes, I certainly do."

"I think they're nuts," Ruth Marshal said.

Krista laughed. "Maybe some of them, but not all of them."

"I suppose not. Miriam Hodge seems capable. Did the pastor defend you?"

"No. He sat there like a lump on a log," Krista said.

"The weasel."

Krista sighed. "I have no idea what I should do. To be honest, I've been thinking how nice it would be to return to teaching."

They sat quietly for a few moments.

"Krista," Ruth said after a while, "I'm not a pastor, but I've thought carefully about the job in my years in the church. For all our vaunted talk about equality, we Quakers often treat our women pastors terribly. Many of our meetings won't even hire a woman, except for a minor role. So the deck is stacked against you from the start. And you've never been married. That, of course, is your business and no one else's. But there will be suspicious souls in every congregation with nothing better to do than speculate about your sexual orientation."

"I'm not a lesbian," Krista said. "I just haven't found the right person. But that's no one's business but my own." She paused for a moment, took another drink of tea, then said reflectively, "There are good people in that congregation. I know there are. Why didn't they speak up?"

"Because they're afraid. People like Fern and Dale think nothing of going on the attack. It is another day's work for them. No one likes to be on the receiving end of that, so nothing is said."

"What should I do?"

"That is not for me to say. But if you're going to stay in ministry, you'll need to be aware of the difficulties and be prepared to deal with them. You'll need to dispose of any rose-colored glasses."

"It shouldn't be that way."

Ruth reached across the table and took her hand. "Krista, dear, many things shouldn't be the way they are. And you will challenge them. And sometimes you will even change things."

"What about the other times?"

"Oh, the other times you'll get run over. But you should try anyway."

It had been a grueling day, and Krista was suddenly aware of being tired. She thanked Ruth, then came around the table to hug her. Ministry wasn't working out the way she'd hoped, but she had met Ruth Marshal, so the venture hadn't been a total loss.

She went upstairs, showered, and climbed into bed. Lying on her back, her hands behind her head, she thought back on her life, trying to recall what she might have done to deserve being pastor to Fern and Dale.

Twenty

Choosing Up Sides

By Monday morning, word had circulated through town about the pastoral bloodbath at Harmony Friends Meeting, and people were choosing up sides—the progressives in support of Krista, the purists, who'd been suspicious of women ministers all along, backing Fern and Dale.

The Sam Gardner household was chilly. When Sam came downstairs after his morning shower, his sons were eating the last of the pancakes and bacon, and Barbara was tugging on her shoes for her morning walk.

"What's for breakfast?" he asked.

"Whatever you want," Barbara said. "Help yourself."

Sam opted for breakfast at the Coffee Cup, where he found a surprising number of his fellow churchmen squeezed into the booths. He pulled up a chair to the end of Ellis Hodge's booth. Ellis was seated with his brother, Ralph, Asa Peacock, and Harvey Muldock.

"Craziest thing I ever saw," Ellis Hodge said. "All I said was that since Sam's dad was doing better, we ought to let Krista go and bring Sam back. Then we wouldn't even be having this trouble, and Miriam dumped my eggs right in the sink."

"Jessie hasn't spoken to me since church," Asa said. "She told me I should have said something since I'm an elder."

"Sounds like she's been talking with my wife," Sam said.

"Eunice is mad at me for mentioning the football game Friday night," Harvey said. "All I did was point out that we had a ball game that night. What was wrong with that?"

Ralph Hodge sipped his coffee.

"Why are you here, Ralph? Sandy mad at you too?" Ellis asked.

"Nope. I'm in charge of my household. I tell my wife how it's going to be, and that's that."

The other men snorted.

"Just don't tell her I said that, or I'll be in the doghouse with the rest of you," Ralph said.

Penny Torricelli stomped over to Sam. "What'll you have and make it snappy. I'm busy this morning."

"And a pleasant good morning to you," Sam said.

"Sam Gardner, you ought to be ashamed of yourself," Penny snapped. "They attack a fine woman, and you sit there on your hands."

"I am on a leave of absence," Sam said. "It would have been inappropriate for me to intrude on the church's business while on leave."

"I knew you'd have some weaselly excuse," Penny said.

"I would like French toast," Sam said. "Warm syrup, no powdered sugar, with a cold glass of milk, which you may bring when my French toast is ready."

He unrolled the napkin around his tableware and smoothed it across his lap, ignoring Penny's glare until she walked away.

"Yeah, it was pretty weaselly, Sam," Asa said. "You should have spoke up for Krista. I didn't say anything because I thought you would."

Ellis Hodge shook his head in disagreement. "No, Sam's right. He's on leave. He shouldn't be buttin' in on the church's business with its pastor. It's not his concern."

"Thank you, Ellis. Those are my feelings exactly."

"Though you probably would have been forgiven if you'd have had the nerve to stand up and defend Krista," Ellis went on. "She did heal your father, after all."

"Asa's right," Harvey said. "You should have said something, Sam. Then we wouldn't have had to meet on Friday night, and I wouldn't be in trouble with my wife."

"That's easy for you guys to say. You have job security. Ellis, you and Asa have your farms. Harvey, you have your garage. I take time off to care for my father, and then when I'm ready to come back to work, you tell me to take another month off. How am I gonna take care of my family when I'm ready to come back and you've decided to get rid of me and hire Krista? Answer me that?"

He crumpled up his napkin and threw it on the table, where it bounced into Harvey's empty plate.

No one said anything.

It occurred to Sam he might have said too much.

He wasn't sure what to do next—leave or change the subject. He was saved from having to decide when Penny brought his French toast and milk.

"Thank you, Penny."

She nodded curtly.

While the others looked on, Sam buttered his French toast, doused it liberally with maple syrup, cut a small piece with the edge of his fork, and ate it, chewing thoughtfully.

Harvey Muldock spoke first. "Boy, I guess we got told."

Sam took another bite, then followed it with a drink of milk.

"What kind of people you think we are?" Ellis asked. "You think we'd get rid of you, just like that? Sure, Krista might give a better sermon than you, but you're our friend. We're not gonna throw you over for somebody else."

Sam reddened, embarrassed.

"Shoot, Sam, we've known you all your life. We wouldn't do you that way," Ellis said.

"Fern and Dale have known me all my life, and they're always trying to get me fired," Sam pointed out.

"Well, that's Fern and Dale. They don't speak for the rest of us," Asa said.

Harvey reached across the booth and punched Sam on the shoulder. "You're stuck with us, buddy. We wouldn't fire you even if you wanted us to."

Sam retrieved his crumpled napkin from Harvey's plate and blew his nose. His eyes felt leaky. "Thank you, Harvey. I appreciate that."

"Yeah, a new preacher might make us toe the line," Asa said. "We'd have to start going to church on Wednesday nights."

"And tithing," Ellis added.

"No telling what would happen with a new preacher," Harvey said. "We'd maybe start growin'. Then we'd have to build a bigger church, and think what that would cost us. Nope, Sam, you suit us just fine."

"Thank you for your vote of confidence, gentlemen. I can't tell you what it means to me," Sam said.

"Let me buy your breakfast, Pastor," Asa said, plucking Sam's bill from underneath his plate.

"You don't have to do that," Sam said.

"I know I don't have to. I want to."

"Then thank you very much."

"I'd love to stay and chat, but I've got corn to pick," Ellis said.

"Me too," Asa said.

"Yep, work's a-waitin'," Harvey said. "How about you, Ralph. What's on your plate today?"

"Thought I'd help my brother with the harvest," Ralph said. "Can you use someone to drive the truck?"

"Sure could," Ellis said.

They bade Sam good-bye, paid their bills, and left the Coffee Cup.

Sam finished his breakfast, wishing he had something to do. After two and a half months of rest, he was thoroughly exhausted and longed for something to keep him occupied. The older he got, the more he became like the people who annoyed him—the folks who couldn't let go, who had to keep their hand in and stir the pot, even when it was someone else's turn. He was a basket case after ten weeks. He hated to think what retirement would do to him. He'd probably end up like Dale and Fern, annoying his peers to no end.

Even though he was officially on leave, he decided to stop past the meetinghouse and visit Frank. He found him at the copier, running off a letter.

"What's that?" Sam asked.

"Miriam asked me to send everyone a letter about this Friday's meeting," Frank said. "I guess it's a church by-law. Members have to be notified by mail or phone call if there isn't time to post a notice in the weekly bulletin."

"Why didn't you just phone everyone? It'd be cheaper."

"Do you want to phone fifty-nine households and have to explain why we're having a meeting and listen to them gripe about having to miss the football game?"

"I see your point."

Sam folded the letters while Frank stuffed the envelopes and licked them shut.

"So what do you think of Krista?" Sam asked.

"I like her just fine. She's really good at impressions."

"Impressions?"

"Yeah, you know, she imitates people. She called me the other day, and I swore it was Opal Majors. She really had me going. And I guess she got Fern Hampton a good one at the Chicken Noodle Dinner," Frank said with a chuckle.

"That's what I heard."

Frank leaned closer to Sam and dropped his voice to a near whisper. "Do you think she is what they say she is?"

"You mean a lesbian?"

Frank nodded.

Sam thought for a moment. "Why does it even matter? Though I can understand why she wouldn't want to say."

"What do you mean?"

"Well, look at it from a pastor's point of view," Sam said. "Fern and Dale and probably a few others think she's homosexual and ought to confess. If she says she is, they'll get her fired. But if she says she isn't, they'll accuse her of lying, and they'll still try to get her fired. The only way to prove them wrong is for her to get married. And she's not going to do that just to please them."

"I'd marry her," Frank said. "I think she's neat."

"I thought you were dating Miss Rudy, you little two-timer."

"There's no ring on this finger yet," Frank said. "Maybe I will ask Krista to marry me. That'd solve the whole problem."

"No, then she'd have another problem," Sam said.

"What's that?"

"She'd be married to an old coot."

"And to think I've missed your company."

Sam laughed.

"I'll tell you one thing," Frank said, turning serious. "I'd like to pop Dale and Fern right in the chops."

"Oh, if it weren't Dale and Fern, it'd be someone else. There's always people who want to think they're better Christians than everyone else, and this is their way of proving it. Pointing the finger at someone else."

"Yeah, I suppose you're right."

They stamped the envelopes, which Sam dropped off at the post office on his way home.

Walking home, Sam was a jumble of feelings. Though grateful for the support of his friends, he knew he'd failed his calling. He wondered how best to remedy the situation, but decided it would be unchristian to knock off Fern and Dale. He decided instead to talk with them the next day, prevailing upon whatever morsel of mercy they might possess.

His mind made up, Sam felt better than he had in weeks. Even though he knew the worst part was still ahead—telling his wife and children they'd been right.

To delay the inevitable, he stopped by his parents' house to visit. Ever since the Chicken Noodle Dinner, his father had been in rare form, a whirling dervish, mowing and painting and digging and organizing. Sam found him cleaning out the garage, which hadn't been done since 1963. His hair was standing on end, crackling with excitement.

"Say, take a look at this, Sam. I forgot I had it." It was a fly rod. "Yep, caught some nice trout with that up in Canada."

"We ought to go fishing, Dad. How about you and I drive up to Canada next week, before I have to go back to work?"

"Are you crazy? Look at this mess. I don't have time to fish. For crying out loud, there's work to be done."

That will be me, Sam thought. Won't take my hand off the tiller.

"Yessiree, too much to do and not enough time to do it," his father said happily, setting the fly rod aside and pushing back into the garage, his day blissfully full.

Twenty-one

The Lines Are Drawn

arbara and the boys accepted Sam's confession with grace and dignity. Barbara fixed fried chicken for dinner and let him have the legs. After supper, they went for a walk around the block, while the boys rode their bicycles, darting around and about like dragonflies. By the time they reached home, the sun had set. A hint of autumn chill lay over the town. Bands of red and orange streaked the sky above Ellis Hodge's silos to the west.

"Red sky at night, sailor's delight," Sam said.

"Red sky in morning, sailors take warning," Barbara finished.

"Looks like tomorrow will be a good day."

"What's on your plate?" Barbara asked.

"I'm going to visit Dale and Fern," Sam said. "And urge them to leave Krista alone."

She slipped her hand in his. "That's the husband I know and love."

Later that evening, after the children were tucked in, Sam and Barbara enjoyed the marital privilege. Making up certainly has its advantages, Sam thought as he fell asleep.

The next morning, he awoke to the scent of oatmeal and sausage wafting through the house. After a quick shower and leisurely breakfast, he walked the boys to school, returning home past Fern Hampton's house, who at that moment, as providence would have it, was pruning a magnolia in front of her home.

"Good morning, Fern," he called out from the sidewalk.

She clipped away, barely turning her head to acknowledge him. "Mornin'."

Lord, give me the right words to say and the right spirit in which to say them, Sam prayed.

"Fern, your yard looks prettier every year. I love your mums. What's your secret?"

"Cow poop."

"Well, I'll have to remember that. Yes, ma'am, I certainly will have to remember that."

She continued snipping here and there, focusing on her task.

He walked up her sidewalk and stood beside her. "Fern, I'm glad I saw you. I'd like to talk with you, if you could spare a moment. It's about Krista."

"You know my thoughts on her. She's not fit to be a minister."

"Fern, there are many people in our meeting who don't agree. If you insist on pursuing this, it will only harm our meeting. I would like you to reconsider."

"It's not up to me," Fern said with a stomp of her foot. "It's in the church's hands now. She wouldn't listen when two of us went to her, so now she must answer to the church."

"Fern, she's new to ministry. This might discourage her from ever following her call."

"Better she finds out now she shouldn't be a pastor."

"That's not for us to say, Fern. She should be given the opportunity to prove herself."

"I gave her the opportunity at the Chicken Noodle Dinner, and she disobeyed me."

Sam girded his loins, swallowed deeply, and plunged ahead.

"That's the real problem, isn't it, Fern? You don't like that she didn't obey you. That's why you don't like her."

"I'll thank you to leave my yard," Fern said, pointing her clippers at Sam in a threatening motion.

Sam could see the headlines now. *Pastor Stabbed with Hedge Clippers by Irate Parishioner.* They certainly hadn't covered this in seminary.

"Fern, I'm shaking the dust from my feet."

"Shake the dust off in your own yard. I don't want it here."

Sam sighed, realizing that his reference to Scripture had gone completely over her head. Subtlety was lost on some people. Maybe he'd have better luck with Dale.

As it turned out, he didn't. Dale tore into him like a tornado, blustery and unrelenting. By the time Sam arrived home he was exhausted, though the day was still new. Prophetic ministry, he was learning, was not for the faint of heart.

He spent the afternoon doing yard work, weeding the flowerbeds and cutting away the spent and wilted summer plants, contemplating his next move. He was not without hope, though that point was fast approaching.

The problem with Matthew 18, Sam finally concluded, was that it assumed goodwill on the part of the offender. Jesus, being a nice guy, believed if matters were presented to people in a straightforward manner, they would do the right thing. It was Sam's opinion that Jesus had died too young and was still in the grip of youthful idealism. Five minutes with Fern and Dale would have doused Jesus's optimism considerably.

Sam mowed his yard, then went next door to mow Shirley Finchum's yard. She had lately been complaining of bad knees. His good deed done for the day, he showered, changed into fresh clothes, and walked the three blocks to the library to return an overdue book.

Miss Rudy went home for supper at five o'clock, leaving a high-school girl to clerk the desk for a half hour. That was the optimal time to return overdue books, when Miss Rudy was gone. Otherwise, you could count on being lectured about the sacred obligations assumed when books were checked out, obligations that included their timely return. Sam could recite her lecture from memory.

Unfortunately, it appeared romance had altered Miss Rudy's timetable. She'd shifted her supper to six o'clock to eat dinner with Frank. She examined the due-date card with a frown.

"I was just getting ready to phone your house, Samuel. We've had requests for this book."

"I'm sorry, Miss Rudy. Time got away from me, what with my father's illness and all."

Sam was never above playing the sympathy card with Miss Rudy, though it seldom helped.

"Honoring one's commitments when life is difficult is the measure of one's character," she said.

"I agree completely. I'm without an excuse."

"Two days overdue at a dime a day. That'll be twenty cents."

Sam handed her two dimes, which she deposited in the metal box she kept in her desk drawer.

"Just helping to pay the electric bill," Sam said, trying to put a positive spin on his delinquency.

"I've not yet forwarded the names of overdue borrowers to Mr. Miles. It would not have reflected well on the church for our minister's name to appear in the newspaper."

"That would have been quite unseemly. I appreciate your restraint, and I will try to do better in the future," Sam promised.

"Will you be checking out any other books today?"

"I don't think so. It's too risky."

"Very well."

Sam stayed to read the magazines, trolling for sermon ideas for when he returned to the pulpit. He was reading the jokes in *Reader's Digest* when he heard muffled voices behind the magazine display. It sounded like Dale Hinshaw and Fern Hampton. He raised the magazine to hide his face and listened closely.

"I got Stanley Farlow to be on our side," Dale said. "But if we win, he wants a room named after his mother."

"Shouldn't be a problem. We could maybe name the basement for her. She was big in the Chicken Noodle Dinner," Fern said. "Shirley Finchum said she'd help us too. Thing is, she doesn't want Sam to come back. She's got a grandson who's a minister, and he needs a job."

"I think Sam's been here long enough," Dale said. "Time for a change, if you ask me."

Sam replaced the magazine and left the library quietly, unsettled by their treachery. What gall, he thought. Ganging up on Krista and now coming after me. And the nerve of Shirley Finchum, plotting my removal after I mowed her yard!

Now it was getting personal.

He arrived home just as Barbara was setting supper on the table. "Wash your hands, boys. Supper's on."

Sam and his sons lined up at the sink, splashed water, and made a general mess of things until their hands were reasonably clean, then sat down at the table. Levi reached for his spoon.

"Wait for your mother," Sam said.

Levi groaned. Barbara took her seat.

"Prayer first. Whose turn is it?" Sam asked.

"Addison's," Levi said.

"I prayed last night. It's your turn," Addison squealed, apparently indignant at the prospect of having to pray two days in a row.

"Actually, I think it's my turn," Sam said. "Let's have Quaker silence."

Sam didn't care for verbal prayers when he was off the clock. They joined hands and bowed their heads. Sam prayed for the grace to forgive Dale and Fern, though without much enthusiasm.

They squeezed hands, picked up their spoons, and began to eat. Chili. And peanut butter and honey sandwiches. One of Sam's top five favorite meals.

"You'll not believe what I overheard at the library," he said, taking a bite of his peanut butter and honey sandwich.

"What?" Barbara asked.

"Dale and Fern plotting against Krista and against me."

"You're kidding."

"Nope," he said. Peanut butter was stuck fast to the roof of his mouth and his speech was garbled. "They've lined up Stanley Farlow and Shirley Finchum on their side, and they want to get me fired so they can hire Shirley's grandson."

"Who's getting tired?" Addison asked.

"No one's tired," Sam said. "I said fired. They want to get me fired."

"Would we have to move?" Levi asked. "I don't want to move. All my friends are here."

"We're not moving anywhere," Barbara said, reaching over to pat Levi's head. "And Daddy won't get fired. We have too many friends at the church."

"I don't like Dale Hinshaw," Addison announced. "Last Sunday, he told me I was bad."

"Don't you pay any attention to him, son," Sam said.

"I wish you weren't a pastor so we didn't have to go to church," Levi said.

"We don't go to church because your father is the pastor," Barbara said. "We go to learn what it means to be grown up."

"You're already grown up. What's there to learn?" Addison asked.

"Well, church teaches us how to forgive and how to help the poor and how to love God and other people," Barbara said.

"So when I learn how to do those things, can I stop going?" Levi asked.

Barbara turned to Sam. "Help me out here, honey."

"You're doing a fine job."

"How was school today?" she asked the boys, changing the subject.

"Levi got in trouble for talking," Addison reported. "He had to stand in the hallway."

"I did not, you doofus. Shut your face."

Sam loved the warm camaraderie of family dinners.

He looked at Levi. "You and I will have a talk after supper, young man."

Insurrection was breaking out all over.

The telephone rang. Sam walked across the kitchen and plucked the phone from the wall. It was Shirley Finchum, all sweetness and light, calling to thank him for mowing her yard. "I don't know what I'd do without you."

"Glad to be of assistance," Sam said. Then, feeling feisty, he added, "I understand you have a grandson who's a minister."

"Yes, that's right. How did you know?"

"I think I heard Fern Hampton mention something about it."

"He got the call just last month, but he doesn't have a church yet."

"When he finds one," Sam said, trying not to snicker, "I hope the people there treat him as kindly as you've always treated me."

Shirley paused. "Well, yes, I suppose so."

"You take care now," Sam said, then hung up.

Barbara grinned at her husband. "That was cruel."

"I thought I let her off pretty easy."

"Can I toilet paper her trees at Halloween?" Levi asked.

"No, young man, you may not TP her house or anyone else's. We don't do that," Barbara said.

"Your mother's right," Sam said. No TPing. You may, however, soap her windows."

"How about I light a bag of cow poop and put it on her porch?" Levi said.

Sam laughed.

"Don't encourage them," Barbara said. "They'll think you're serious."

"No TP, no soap, no cow poop," Sam said solemnly. "And no more talking in school when you're supposed to be quiet. Understand?"

"Yes, sir."

Sam wished all rebellion was so easily suppressed.

Their night ended quietly, a calm before the storm Sam knew to be brewing.

Twenty-two

Sam Redeems Himself

Krista Riley had been preoccupied all week, antici-
pating Friday evening and the termination of her
brief career as a pastor. Thursday morning found her
seated in class, listening to a professor drone on about the
Hittites and the Ammonites, people long dead and of little
concern to her or any of the seminarians around her, most
of whom were dozing or working that morning's crossword
puzzle.

Studying ancient animosities was of some consolation; it
helped her put her own struggles in perspective. It wasn't as if
human strife were a modern trend. She would face other chal-
lenges in the future, and this one would fade from memory.
She kept telling herself that, but the knot in her stomach didn't
lessen, and she dreaded Friday's meeting more each hour.

After lunch, she was summoned to Dean Mullen's office. He
was seated behind his desk, smiling pleasantly. "Welcome, welcome. Come in, come in." Krista went on guard immediately,

having learned that when Dean Mullen repeated himself, bad news was often at hand.

"Sit down, sit down," he said.

She sat in the chair beside his desk.

"Well, well," he said, leaning back in his chair, smiling. "How are things working out for you in Harmony?"

Krista considered how best to answer. "It's a curious place," she said after a moment's pause.

Dean Mullen chuckled. "Yes, yes. You can say that again. You sure can say that again."

Krista's dread deepened. A double repeat. This couldn't be good.

"I got a phone call from Miriam Hodge this morning. She mentioned you'd hit a bit of a rough patch."

"You might say that," Krista said.

Dean Mullen studied his calendar. "There are two weeks remaining in your ministry there. Wouldn't it be easier just to quit?"

"Yes, I suppose it would," Krista said. "But I'm not going to."

Dean Mullen smiled. "That's the spirit. Hang in there with them. That's what I've always said. Hang in there with them."

He hesitated and then said, "Miriam said several of the members have accused you of being a lesbian."

"That's right."

"And that you've refused to say one way or the other."

Krista smiled. "Actually, I told them it was none of their business."

Dean Mullen laughed a deep, rich laugh. "Good for you. Good for you. If you cave in to tyranny, there'll be no end to it." He stood up behind his desk and walked around to Krista, placing a hand on her shoulder. "Krista Riley, you are going to make some church somewhere a wonderful pastor. You are strong and self-confident, but also kind."

Krista was flooded with warmth. "Thank you, Dean. Thank you."

Now I'm repeating myself, she thought. It must be contagious.

"Don't mention it," Dean Mullen said. "Don't mention it."

She made her way to the door, then paused when the dean asked, "What's Sam Gardner doing in all of this?"

"To be truthful, not much," Krista said.

"Huh, that surprises me," Dean Mullen said with a frown. "Sam is usually a pretty good egg. You want me to phone him? Ask him to put in a good word for you? Maybe goose him along a bit?"

Krista thought for a moment. "No, I think I need to stand on my own two feet."

"You do that then. And we'll be praying for you. God's peace and strength to you, friend."

She left the dean's office elated, feeling more alive than she had in years.

Back in Harmony, Sam spent the morning helping his mother wash windows and discussing the upcoming showdown. He didn't disclose what he'd overheard in the library. His mother, he had learned over the years, was not the most objective person when it came to Sam and his detractors. He didn't want to see her engaged in fisticuffs with Fern Hampton.

After a lunch of grilled cheese sandwiches and tomato soup, Sam stopped by the meetinghouse to visit with Frank, whom he caught dozing in his chair.

"You better get all the rest you can now," Sam told him. "When I'm back in charge of things, you'll be too busy to slack off."

Frank groaned and rubbed his eyes.

"What's the matter?" Sam asked. "Miss Rudy keeping you up too late?"

"Shush up, you young whippersnapper."

Sam enjoyed Frank, if only because it made him feel young to be called a whippersnapper or any of the other colorful names Frank regularly bestowed on him, such as hooligan, lout, and ruffian.

Sam wheeled his chair into Frank's office and sat down, propping his feet on the edge of Frank's desk. "Anything new?"

"Fern Hampton stopped by."

"What's our old friend Fern up to?" Sam asked.

"Seems she wants to bring in Shirley Finchum's grandson to replace you."

"Yes, I heard something about that."

"And," Frank said, smiling broadly, "she said if I backed her, she'd make sure I stayed on as secretary and got a raise."

"Well, that little scalawag," Sam said. "Of all the nerve."

After he told Frank about the conversation he'd overheard

between Fern and Dale, Frank asked, "Shirley Finchum and Stanley Farlow are in on it too?"

"It appears so."

"I've never trusted the Finchums or the Farlows. They're ne'er-do-wells!"

"Good-for-nothings!"

"Malingerers!" Frank said.

"Idlers!"

They collapsed in a fit of laughter, giggling like two schoolgirls.

"You gonna be at the meeting?" Sam asked.

"Are you kidding? I wouldn't miss it for the world. I think we oughta sell tickets. I saw Clevis Nagle at the Coffee Cup this morning, and he asked if he could come and he's not even a member."

It occurred to Sam they weren't exhibiting the proper gravity for such an occasion, but after his anxieties about losing his job, it felt good to laugh.

"What did you tell him?"

"I told him there probably wouldn't be room, but that he could purchase the video for twenty dollars."

"What?"

"Sure, why not? Besides, if we tape it, we'll have it on record. You know how Fern is. We have a meeting to decide something and if she doesn't get her way, she just keeps hammering away, claiming we'd never made a decision one way or the other, until she gets her way. If we tape it, we'll have her dead to rights."

"Good thinking," Sam said. "Okay, you can tape it. But you can't sell it."

"Not even if we give the money to Brother Norman's shoe ministry to the Choctaw Indians?"

Sam frowned. "No, not even then. It isn't seemly."

"You're the boss," Frank said.

"Maybe not now," Sam said, standing to leave, "but in another couple weeks. Then you'll have to stop all your goofing off and do some real work."

"You never know what Quakers will do. We might decide to keep Krista on and give you the heave-ho. I wouldn't be picking colors for your office just yet."

Sam chuckled. He'd missed bickering with Frank.

He stopped past the newspaper on his way home to pick up that week's edition of the *Harmony Herald*. He plucked a paper from the wire rack outside the front door, depositing a quarter in the canister. He walked over to the bench on the sidewalk, sat down, and glanced at the front page.

Local Church on Verge of Split! it read. The article went on at length, spilling over to the back page, describing the controversy over Krista, naming names and generally sparing readers no detail.

Sam groaned.

"Pretty good piece of reporting, if I do say so myself," Bob Miles said, standing behind him.

"I wish you hadn't done this, Bob. It's just gonna make folks upset."

"What do you mean? Everybody knows anyway. Might as well write about it. In fact, I'm thinking of starting up a new weekly column on the church fights in this town. One week I could write about the Catholics fighting, then the Baptists, then the Quakers. Now that would sell some papers."

"There are things here only the elders knew," Sam said, deeply perturbed. "Who spilled the beans?"

"I never reveal a source," Bob said loftily.

"I can't imagine the Friendly Women will be happy to see this. They'll probably pull their ad for next year's Chicken Noodle Dinner," Sam said.

"Okay, it was Fern Hampton and Dale Hinshaw. They told me everything," Bob said, his ethics crumbling under the threat of economic pressure.

"I knew it. I knew it was them. The big blabbermouths."

"Don't tell them I told you," Bob said. "They'll never tell me anything again."

Sam read the rest of the paper, seething over Dale and Fern. The nerve of them, revealing confidential matters discussed in the elders meetings, Sam thought. Unfortunately, the elders at Harmony Friends, with the exception of Miriam Hodge, regularly blabbed the church's business all over town. If a lack of discretion were grounds for dismissal, Sam would have to fire half the church.

He folded the paper, tucking it under his arm, then walked the three blocks home down Washington Street. Barbara was in the kitchen, folding laundry on the table. She greeted Sam with a kiss, then said, "Miriam Hodge just called. She wants you to call her."

"Bad news?"

"She didn't say. She just wanted you to call her as soon as you got in."

Sam dialed her number, listening to the three short rings of Miriam's line. The Hodges were on a party line, which they shared with three neighbors. Whenever he spoke with Miriam, he could hear Leota Stout's muffled breathing as she listened in.

Miriam picked up the phone.

"Hi, Miriam. It's Sam, returning your call."

"Hello, Sam. Thanks for calling back."

They listened quietly. Leota Stout coughed.

"Leota, I believe the phone's for me, dear. Would you mind hanging up?" Miriam said.

The phone line clicked.

"What's up?" Sam asked.

"Sam, I feel terrible telling you this, but I can't make tomorrow's meeting."

"Is everything all right?"

"Not really. My sister phoned this morning, and she's having an operation tomorrow. She asked if I could come help her. She doesn't have anyone else, and I couldn't tell her no."

Sam stifled a sigh. This was disastrous. Miriam Hodge was often the only reason the church didn't descend into total lunacy. There was no telling what would happen with her gone.

"Of course you need to go be with her," Sam said charitably. "She's your sister."

"I'm sorry, Sam. I know I'm letting you and Krista down, but it can't be helped."

"I'm sure she'll understand, Miriam. Don't you worry about it. You just take good care of your sister."

"Thank you, Sam. I appreciate your understanding." Miriam paused. "I know this is irregular, but I'm on my way out the door now. I tried phoning Krista, but she wasn't home. She must still be in class. Would you mind phoning her and explaining my predicament?"

"Not at all," Sam lied. "I'd be happy to do it."

Embarrassed by his reluctance to come to Krista's aid earlier, he'd been avoiding her, but now contact seemed inevitable.

"Do you happen to have her number?" he asked.

Miriam recited it, and Sam wrote it down, assuring her he would call.

He phoned her that evening, after the boys were in bed. She picked up on the second ring. "Hi, Krista. Sam Gardner here."

He didn't ask her how she was doing for fear she would tell him.

"Just wanted to touch base with you before the meeting tomorrow. Miriam Hodge tried calling you earlier. She won't be able to be there. Her sister's in the hospital. But she wanted to tell you not to worry."

Krista sighed. "That's not good. I was counting on Miriam's support."

"I'm going to be there."

Krista hesitated. "I don't mean to sound ungrateful, but you've been pretty quiet through all of this. I've been waiting for you to say something."

"About that," Sam said, swallowing hard, then plunging ahead, "you're absolutely right. I should have spoken up for you when all this started. The truth is, I've been rather jealous. You're so gifted, and people seemed so enamored with you. I was afraid of losing my job to you."

Krista didn't say anything at first. Sam thought they'd been disconnected. "Krista, are you still there?"

"Yes, I'm still here. Sam, when I came to your church, it was with the understanding that I would only be there three months. Even if the meeting had offered me your job, I wouldn't have taken it."

"I'm sorry I didn't trust you," Sam said. "And I want you to know that I'll make it up to you. If they fire you, I'm gone too."

He said it without thinking, grew slightly panicked by his promise, but resolved inwardly to honor it.

Krista chuckled. "Don't do that, Sam. I only have two more weeks to go. It's not worth quitting over. You have a family to support. Let's just not make it easy for them to fire me. Okay?"

"You got it," Sam said.

They chatted a few minutes more. When Sam finally hung up the phone, he felt much better. Regaining one's integrity was never easy, but it paid handsome dividends, and he went to sleep, confident that no matter what happened the next day he would at the very least not be a weasel.

Twenty-three

The Showdown

Friday morning dawned clear. Outside Sam and Barbara's bedroom window, the sun struck the red maple, turning it to fire. He blinked awake and rolled over to hold her, but her side of the bed was empty. He could hear her bustling about downstairs as she got the boys ready for school. He swung his feet over the side of the bed, blinked his eyes to clear the cobwebs, and donned his robe and slippers.

Barbara was standing at the counter mixing pancake batter, Levi was setting the table, and Addison was curled up in the chair beside the woodstove in their kitchen, entertaining the breakfast crowd by reading aloud from a *Calvin and Hobbes* cartoon book.

After a leisurely breakfast, Sam took a shower and dressed. Then he and Barbara walked the boys to school.

"You think many folks will come to the meeting tonight?" Barbara asked on their way home.

"It'll be packed," Sam predicted. "Fern and Dale have been working hard to fill the place with sympathizers."

"I can't believe this is happening in a Friends meeting," Barbara said, shaking her head.

"It's annoying," Sam said, "but not surprising. Some of those folks not only don't know what it means to be Quaker, they don't care to know. We ought to change our sign to read *Harmony Almost Friends Meeting*."

Barbara chuckled. "That would be closer to the truth." She turned toward him. "Have you decided whether you're going to speak tonight?"

"Yep. Haven't figured out what I'm going to say, but I'm going to say something."

"That's my Sam," she said, squeezing his hand.

The day sped past. After a light supper, Sam and Barbara and the boys left for the meeting at six-thirty. Church being free and the football game costing four dollars, people looking for excitement at a bargain were filling the meetinghouse. Longtime members, displaced from their customary pews by Baptists and Catholics, were flitting about in a tizzy. Fern Hampton arrived to find Ned Kivett and the extended Kivett clan residing in her pew and had cleared it within thirty seconds, knocking them aside like bowling pins.

Krista entered the meeting room at five before seven. The chatter subsided as people grew aware of her presence. She walked by herself to a pew up front. Sam and his family rose from their seats and went to sit with her.

With Miriam Hodge absent, the task of leading the meeting had fallen to Asa Peacock, a nice man in Sam's opinion, though a life spent wading through manure seemed poor preparation for the niceties of ecclesial dialogue. At seven o'clock, Asa stood and made his way to the front of the meeting room to stand at the pulpit. Normally reticent, he became talkative when nervous.

"Well, I guess with Miriam gone to take care of her sister, it falls to me to get things started. We're here because Fern and Dale think Krista is, uh, well, how should I say this, uh, not quite right in the sex department. And she won't say one way or the other, even though it sure would make our jobs easier if she did. Now there are some folks who think she's not fit to be a pastor, but other folks who like her, so we're just gonna settle this nice and fair and take a vote."

Sam raised his hand.

"Yeah, Sam. What's on your mind?"

"Asa, I know you're in charge and I don't mean to tell you what to do, but Quakers don't vote."

Asa blushed. "Oh, that's right. Sorry about that, folks. Well then, I guess we'll just talk things over and see what we come up with. Who wants to go first?"

Shirley Finchum grasped the pew in front of her and hauled herself upward. "I say we get rid of her. She's been here long enough, and so has Sam," she said, her appreciation for Sam's lawn-care assistance apparently fading.

"That girl's been nothing but trouble since she got here," Fern said, lunging to her feet, scattering Kivetts in her wake. "She's split the Friendly Women right down the middle. We got along fine until she came."

Sam leaned over to Krista. "Try not to take it personally," he said. "I'm sure they don't mean it."

"Firing's too good for her," Dale Hinshaw screeched. "We need to cast her out of the church altogether."

"I, for one, appreciate Krista and her ministry," Judy Iverson said. "As for her sexual orientation, I don't think that's any of our business."

"Judy's right," Deena Morrison said. "We've not asked anyone else what we're asking her."

"I liked the tea she made at the Chicken Noodle Dinner," Harvey Muldock said. "I've been telling Eunice for years they needed to sweeten it up."

"The tea was good," Asa agreed.

"We all got along in this church just fine until she got here," Stanley Farlow said. "Now we're fightin' with one another. I'm just glad my mother isn't alive to see this."

"I knew he'd work his mother into this somehow," Barbara whispered to Sam.

Sam sat quietly, contemplating Stanley Farlow's mother, who, had she been alive, would have called for Krista's public flogging.

"I suppose we ought to ask Krista if she wants to speak," Asa Peacock said.

Silence fell across the meeting room. People turned toward Krista, expectantly. After a few moments, she rose and turned to face the congregation.

"Ever since I was a little girl, I've wanted to be a pastor. It's all I've ever wanted. Of course, when you're Roman Catholic and female, that's pretty hard to do," she said, smiling. "So I became a teacher instead. But still my dream was to be a minister, to have a church like this one where I could help people and serve God. Then the way opened for me to come and be with you, and I was so happy."

She paused, as if weighing whether to continue, then spoke again. "Every generation of the church has its struggle. Our parents had to decide whether to include people of color. Today, the church is locked in a debate about whether homosexuals can belong. Your preoccupation with my sexuality leads to nothing good. If I tell you I'm straight, you'll let me stay, though some of you would still wonder about me and treat me poorly. If I tell you I'm homosexual, I would not be welcome. No matter how I answer your question, one thing remains unchanged—gay people are not welcome here."

All across the meeting room, people hung their heads, embarrassed. Dale Hinshaw looked about, panicked, seeming to sense the tide was shifting in Krista's favor. "Matthew 18 is clear. She's refusing to cooperate. She needs to be to us as a tax collector and a Gentile."

Oscar Purdy plunged an index finger in his ear to adjust his hearing aid. "What'd he say about raising our taxes?" he asked his wife.

Fern Hampton stood again to speak. "Don't let her distract you from the real matter. We've asked her a simple question on a matter of great consequence to the church. She's refused to answer it. If we suspected her of stealing money from the church and she didn't answer our questions, we'd fire her. Why is this any different?"

"She's got a point there," Ned Kivett said to his wife.

The Quakers sat quietly, weighing Fern's words.

Sam closed his eyes, recalling what Miss Rudy had told him that week at the library. "Honoring one's commitments when life is difficult is the measure of one's character."

Years ago, Sam had sat in this very room and made a commitment to the Lord to be a minister worthy of that high calling, to comfort the afflicted and afflict the comfortable. Dear God, give me the words to say, he prayed silently, then rose to his feet.

He surveyed the room, taking measure of who was there. Almost everyone who meant anything to him was present—his wife and sons, his parents, his friends, his flock.

"I'm glad you're here tonight. This is an important day for our church. Because tonight we get to decide what kind of church we're going to be. Not every congregation gets that chance. Most days in the church are business as usual, not at all that much hangs in the balance. But not today. Today we get to decide what kind of church we're going to be."

He paused, gathering his thoughts.

"Something here tonight doesn't feel right to me. I can't quite define it, I just know how it makes me feel: sad. Sad that somewhere along the line we missed the boat. Instead of figuring out how best to prepare Krista for ministry, we've met to judge her. We got suspicious and asked her a question we've never asked anyone else in this church. We've asked Krista to tell us about her sex life and defended our right to know because she is a pastor. But in all my years of ministry, not one person has ever asked me about my sex life."

Across the room, Dale Hinshaw frowned at the mention of sex.

"But since we're all so curious to know about our pastors' sex lives, I think we ought to start with mine. There's something about me you don't know. Something I kept secret for years. There was a certain Sausage Queen—I won't name her name—whom I was infatuated with. I never told anyone and never acted on it, but I had thoughts about her, thoughts that weren't appropriate."

Barbara stared at him, an odd look on her face.

What he said next came as an utter surprise to him and everyone else in the meeting room. "So if we're going to get rid of anyone around here, it should be me."

He sat down, worried they'd follow his suggestion, but also feeling strangely free.

Shirley Finchum fanned herself vigorously, utterly appalled. "I agree. Let's give him the heave-ho."

"I bet he had the hots for Nora Nagle," Ned Kivett said to Kyle Weathers.

"Can't fault him there," Kyle whispered back.

Across the meeting room, Judy Iverson rose to her feet. "Sam is right. Tonight we get to decide what kind of church we're going to be. Are we going to be a church where people are accepted and loved and forgiven, or are we going to be a church with no room in our pews for folks who've fallen short or are a little different?"

"Be ye perfect," Dale Hinshaw piped up, "even as your Father in heaven is perfect."

"Let him who is without sin cast the first stone," Gloria Gardner said, fixing Dale with a glare.

Asa Peacock went to the pulpit. "Anybody else have something to say?"

"I think the Lord's telling us to purify ourselves, and it needs to start with our leaders," Fern Hampton said. "A church is only as good as its leadership."

"Amen to that," Dale said.

Frank snorted. "If the Lord's telling us to do something, how come the rest of us aren't hearing it?"

Asa studied the congregation in an effort to gauge their sentiments. "Seems like there's only a few folks who want Krista and Sam to go. So as near as I can figure, we ought to keep them on. Do folks agree?"

"Agreed," the congregation replied, except for Fern and her minions.

"I don't agree," Fern said. "I don't agree one bit."

"Well, I suppose you can bring it up at next month's business meeting," Asa said.

"She'll be gone by then," Fern whined, clearly distressed the church wasn't doing all it could to make Krista's life miserable.

Asa elected not to respond. He glanced at his watch. "Friends, if we hurry, we can catch the second half of the football game."

The crowd dispersed quickly, except for Fern and Dale, who huddled with their few allies at the back of the meeting room, clearly distressed by this outburst of common sense and grace.

Krista turned to Sam. "Thank you, Sam. That was very kind of you. And brave. Not many pastors would have the courage to confess such a thing."

Sam beamed, thoroughly pleased with himself.

Barbara tugged on his sleeve. "Come on, lover boy," she said brusquely.

"See you, Sunday," Sam said to Krista. "I'm looking forward to your message."

"Thanks again, Sam. It was awfully kind of you."

"Don't mention it," he said magnanimously. "Glad I could help."

It was a quiet walk home. Barbara hurried the boys along to bed. She stood over them while they brushed their teeth, then hurriedly read them a story.

She came downstairs to find Sam reading in his easy chair.

"Now what's this about you having the hots for a Sausage Queen?" she asked, a slight edge to her voice.

Sam, sensing for the first time he might be in trouble, grinned weakly. "Pretty clever, wasn't it? I thought I'd show them that some matters were private, sex being one of them."

"Why didn't you just say that?"

"Not my fault," Sam said. "Right before I stood up, I asked the Lord to give me the words to say and those were the words He gave me. You'll have to take the matter up with Him."

"Oh, brother."

"Can't have it both ways," Sam said. "You got mad when I didn't defend Krista. Now I speak and you're angry."

"I suppose I'll get over it. I just wished you had exercised more discretion."

She whacked him with a rolled-up newspaper. Fortunately, it was the *Herald* and not the *New York Times* Sunday edition, so it didn't hurt.

"You really think about the Sausage Queens?"

"It was a long time ago," Sam said. "And I've thought about you a lot more. And I never acted on it and never would."

"You better never, mister, or you won't be able to have a sex life. Is that clear?"

"Crystal," Sam said.

Later that night, in bed, Barbara scooted beside him and rested her head on his shoulder. "You're a bozo," she said affectionately.

"Yep."

"What do you think will happen to Krista?"

"I think she'll go on to make some church a fine pastor. She'll probably be my superintendent some day."

"Wonder what Dale and Fern will do?"

"Probably move on to other endeavors, like tormenting orphans and widows."

They fell asleep that way, Sam on his back, his arm around Barbara, her leg draped over his, in the steady, familiar way husbands and wives have with each other when their love is deep enough to forgive the occasional fantasy, so long as it doesn't become a habit.

Twenty-four

A Grand Slam

T he next morning, Sam went for a haircut at Kyle's.

"Still married?" Kyle asked, as he snipped around Sam's ears.

"Happily."

"I don't believe I'd have publicly confessed to hankerin' after a Sausage Queen. Some things you ought to keep to yourself."

"You might have a point there," Sam agreed. "Though I guess the proof is in the pudding. Krista and I still have our jobs."

"Can't argue with success, I suppose."

Kyle shaved the back of Sam's neck, clipped a wayward hair sprouting from his right ear, then dusted his neck with talcum.

Kyle stepped back to inspect him. "Want you to look your best now that you're going back to work. Wouldn't do to have a shaggy pastor."

Work. The word fell sweetly on Sam's ear. He'd missed it. Missed waking up each day with a purpose, with some noble venture to engage him. He'd end up like Harvey Muldock and Fern Hampton, people who couldn't let go, lest the world forget them. Three months off the job had nearly ruined him. He couldn't imagine what retirement would do to him.

He spent the day raking leaves, lining them up in long piles along the driveway, then setting a match to them. The wind, he noted with some satisfaction, carried the smoke toward Shirley Finchum's laundry hanging on the clothesline.

He and Barbara and the boys arrived at the meetinghouse fifteen minutes before the start of worship, just in time for donuts and coffee. He greeted Fern and Dale warmly—victory had made him charitable toward his foes. A few people, those who believed pastors should be sinless, kept their distance from him. But everyone else seemed genuinely glad to see him.

While Sam was in seminary, his professor of preaching told him, "You won't hit a home run every week, but always try to advance the runners." That Sunday morning, Krista hit a grand slam. She spoke on forgiveness, and her words soared; her sincere and gracious manner added to the luster. Sam had often joked with Barbara that he'd become a minister so he wouldn't have to listen to other pastors preach. But he could have listened to Krista all day.

After her message, she sat down, and silence enveloped them. Sam's mind turned back over the past four months. He remembered Brother Lester, the one-legged evangelist, coming to revive them, how Dale had seized the reins of evangelism, alienating the entire town and nearly killing his father. Yet, in the words of the Apostle Paul, it had all worked together for good. Krista had come to their shores, teaching them much about dignity, courage, and grace.

When Dale had invited Brother Lester to bring them revival, this likely hadn't been the new life Dale had envisioned. But then it was never wise to constrain the ways of God. The Spirit blew where it wished—one day a balmy breeze, the next a burly blast, sweeping clean the soul of all its hard debris.

A NOTE TO MY FRIENDS

When I was a child, I spent a lot of time in the woods, dreaming of becoming a forest ranger when I grew up. Forest rangers, it seemed to me, lived an idyllic life, freed from the clinch of church and school. I most certainly did not want to become a pastor. I could barely tolerate the one hour a week my parents made me attend. As for school, I was a flop, failing one subject after another, and not just barely, but spectacularly, like a spiraling plane, its engines crippled, smashing headlong into the ground. I despised English and composition most of all. The parts of a sentence were, and remain, a mystery to me. I wouldn't recognize a pluperfect predicate if it kicked me in the shins.

And so God, in that whimsical way of the Divine, determined I should spend my life pastoring and writing.

The pastoring came first. In 1983, I became the youth minister at Plainfield Friends Meeting in Indiana. It has always mystified me why churches allow novice pastors to practice on their most vulnerable members. I've always thought new ministers should train with the elderly, who are not as easily corrupted. But the experience was a fine one and I made many friends.

In 1990, I became the pastor of Irvington Friends Meeting in Indianapolis. There were twelve people in the congregation and their first request of me was to start a newsletter, even though I could have phoned everyone with the news in five minutes. I knew nothing about writing, so returned to college, to the Earlham School of Religion, where I sat at the feet of Tom Mullen, one night a week for a year. Those newsletter essays became my first book, *Front Porch Tales*. You're holding my thirteenth book in your hands. Thirteen, for the superstitious-minded, is unlucky. But I'm not turned that way and feel nothing but blessed.

I continue to pastor, serving as the co-pastor of Fairfield Friends Meeting near Indianapolis. If you're ever in the area, stop by and visit. I venture out occasionally to give a talk or visit a bookstore, where I meet my readers, many of whom have become my friends.

If you're interested, here are some ways we can get to know one another a little better:

If you have e-mail, I can be contacted at *info@philipgulleybooks.com*.

If you're old-fashioned, you can send a letter to me at Harper-SanFrancisco, 353 Sacramento Street, Suite 500, San Francisco, CA 94111-3653. They'll forward your letter to me and I'll answer it, just as my mother and father taught me.

If you're reading one of my books in your book club and would like me to phone in for a visit, write to *info@philipgulleybooks.com* and we'll get the ball rolling.

If you would like me to speak at an event, contact Mr. David Leonards at *ieb@prodigy.net* or (317) 926-7566.

Thank you for buying and reading my books. I derive much joy in writing them; it is my prayer that you find joy in reading them.

Take care.

Philip Gulley

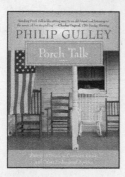